Clive Barker was born in Liverpool in 1952. He is the author of The Books of Blood (in six volumes), The Damnation Game, Weaveworld, Cabal, The Great and Secret Show and Imajica.

He also writes, directs and produces for the screen. His films include Hellraiser and Nightbreed.

He lives in Los Angeles.

Clive Barker's Books of Blood

volume IV

CLIVE BARKER

Every body is a book of blood;
Wherever we're opened, we're red.

SPHERE BOOKS LIMITED

A *Sphere* Book

First published in Great Britain in 1985 by Sphere Books
Reprinted 1987, 1988, 1989, 1991, 1993

ISBN 0 7221 1373 0

Printed in England by Clays Ltd, St Ives plc

Sphere Books
A Division of
Macdonald & Co (Publishers)
165 Great Dover Street
London SE1 4YA

To Alec and Con

ACKNOWLEDGEMENTS

My thanks to: Doug Bennett, who got me into Pentonville – and out again – in the same day, and later furnished me with his insights on prisons and the prison service; to Jim Burr, for his mind's eye tour of White Deer, Texas, and for the New York adventures; to Ros Stanwell-Smith, for her enthusiastic detailing of plagues and how to start them; and to Barbara Boote, my tireless editor, whose enthusiasm has proved the best possible spur to invention.

CONTENTS

THE BODY POLITIC

WHENEVER HE WOKE, Charlie George's hands stood still.

Perhaps he would be feeling too hot under the blankets, and have to throw a couple over to Ellen's side of the bed. Perhaps he might even get up, still half-asleep, and pad through to the kitchen to pour himself a tumbler of iced apple-juice. Then back to bed, slipping in beside Ellen's gentle crescent, to let sleep drift over him. They'd wait then; until his eyes had flickered closed and his breathing become regular as clockwork, and they were certain he was sound asleep. Only then, when they knew consciousness was gone, would they dare to begin their secret lives again.

For months now Charlie had been waking up with an uncomfortable ache in his wrists and hands.

'Go and see a doctor,' Ellen would tell him, unsympathetic as ever. 'Why won't you go and see a doctor?'

1

He hated doctors, that was why. Who in their right mind would trust someone who made a profession out of poking around in sick people?

'I've probably been working too hard,' he told himself.

'Some chance,' Ellen muttered.

Surely that was the likeliest explanation? He was a packager by trade; he worked with his hands all day long. They got tired. It was only natural.

'Stop fretting, Charlie,' he told his reflection one morning as he slapped some life into his face, 'your hands are fit for anything.'

So, night after night, the routine was the same. It goes like this:

The Georges are asleep, side by side in their marital bed. He on his back, snoring gently; she curled up on his left-hand side. Charlie's head is propped up on two thick pillows. His jaw is slightly ajar, and beneath the vein-shot veil of his lids his eyes scan some dreamed adventure. Maybe a fire-fighter tonight, perhaps a heroic dash into the heart of some burning brothel. He dreams contentedly, sometimes frowning, sometimes smirking.

There is a movement under the sheet. Slowly, *cautiously* it seems, Charlie's hands creep up out of the warmth of the bed and into the open air. Their index fingers weave like nailed heads as they meet on his undulating abdomen. They clasp each other in greeting, like comrades-in-arms. In his sleep Charlie moans. The brothel has collapsed on him. The hands flatten themselves instantly, pretending innocence. After a moment, once the even rhythm of his breathing has resumed, they begin their debate in earnest.

A casual observer, sitting at the bottom of the Georges' bed, might take this exchange as a sign of some mental disorder in Charlie. The way his hands

2

twitch and pluck at each other, stroking each other now, now seeming to fight. But there's clearly some code or sequence in their movements, however spasmodic. One might almost think that the slumbering man was deaf and dumb, and talking in his sleep. But the hands are speaking no recognizable sign-language; nor are they trying to communicate with anyone but each other. This is a clandestine meeting, held purely between Charlie's hands. There they will stay, through the night, perched on his stomach, plotting against the body politic.

Charlie wasn't entirely ignorant of the sedition that was simmering at his wrists. There was a fumbling suspicion in him that something in his life was not quite right. Increasingly he had the sense of being cut off from common experience: becoming more and more a spectator to the daily (and nightly) rituals of living, rather than a participator. Take, for example, his love-life.

He had never been a great lover, but neither did he feel he had anything to apologize for. Ellen seemed satisfied with his attentions. But these days he felt dislocated from the act. He would watch his hands travelling over Ellen, touching her with all the intimate skill they knew, and he would view their manoeuvres as if from a great distance, unable to enjoy the sensations of warmth and wetness. Not that his digits were any less agile. Quite the reverse. Ellen had recently taken to kissing his fingers, and telling him how clever they were. Her praise didn't reassure him one iota. If anything, it made him feel worse, to think that his hands were giving such pleasure when he was feeling nothing.

There were other signs of his instability too. Small, irritating signs. He had become conscious of how his fingers beat out martial rhythms on the boxes he was sealing up at the factory, and the way his hands had

3

taken to breaking pencils, snapping them into tiny pieces before he realized quite what he (they) were doing, leaving shards of wood and graphite scattered across the packing room floor.

Most embarrassingly, he had found himself holding hands with total strangers. This had happened on three separate occasions. Once in a taxi-rank, and twice in the lift at the factory. It was, he told himself, nothing more than the primitive urge to hold on to another person in a changing world; that was the best explanation he could muster. Whatever the reason, it was damned disconcerting, especially when he found himself surreptitiously holding hands with his own foreman. Worse still, the other man's hand had grasped Charlie's in return, and the men had found themselves looking down their arms like two dog-owners watching their unruly pets copulating at the ends of their leashes.

Increasingly, Charlie had taken to peering at the palms of his hands, looking for hair. That was the first sign of madness, his mother had once warned him. Not the hair, the looking.

Now it became a race against time. Debating on his belly at night, his hands knew very well how critical Charlie's state of mind had become; it could only be a matter of days before his careering imagination alighted on the truth.

So what to do? Risk an early severance, with all the possible consequences; or let Charlie's instability take its own, unpredictable, course, with the chance of his discovering the plot on his way to madness? The debates became more heated. Left, as ever, was cautious: 'What if we're wrong,' it would rap, 'and there's no life after the body?'

'Then we will never know,' Right would reply.

4

Left would ponder that problem a moment. Then: 'How will we do it, when the time comes?'

It was a vexing question and Left knew it troubled the leader more than any other. 'How?' it would ask again, pressing the advantage. 'How? How?'

'We'll find a way,' Right would reply. 'As long as it's a clean cut.'

'Suppose he resists?'

'A man resists with his hands. His hands will be in revolution against him.'

'And which of us will it be?'

'He uses me most effectively,' Right would reply, 'so I must wield the weapon. You will go.'

Left would be silent a while then. They had never been apart, all these years. It was not a comfortable thought.

'Later, you can come back for me,' Right would say.

'I will.'

'You *must*. I am the Messiah. Without me there will be nowhere to go. You must raise an army, then come and fetch me.'

'To the ends of the earth, if necessary.'

'Don't be sentimental.'

Then they'd embrace, like long-lost brothers, swearing fidelity forever. Ah, such hectic nights, full of the exhilaration of planned rebellion. Even during the day, when they had sworn to stay apart, it was impossible sometimes not to creep together in an idle moment and tap each other. To say:

Soon, soon,

to say:

Again tonight: I'll meet you on his stomach,

to say:

What will it be like, when the world is ours?

Charlie knew he was close to a nervous breakdown. He found himself glancing down at his hands on occasion, to watch them with their index fingers in the air like the heads of long-necked beasts, sensing the horizon. He found himself staring at the hands of other people in his paranoia, becoming obsessed with the way hands spoke a language of their own, independent of their user's intentions. The seductive hands of the virgin secretary, the maniacal hands of a killer he saw on the television, protesting his innocence. Hands that betrayed their owners with every gesture, contradicting anger with apology, and love with fury. They seemed to be everywhere, these signs of mutiny. Eventually he knew he had to speak to somebody before he lost his sanity.

He chose Ralph Fry from Accounting: a sober, uninspiring man, whom Charlie trusted. Ralph was very understanding.

'You get these things,' he said. 'I got them when Yvonne left me. Terrible nervous fits.'

'What did you do about it?'

'Saw a headshrinker. Name of Jeudwine. You should try some therapy. You'll be a changed man.'

Charlie turned the idea over in his mind. 'Why not?' he said after a few revolutions. 'Is he expensive?'

'Yes. But he's good. Got rid of my twitches for me: no trouble. I mean, 'til I went to him I thought I was your average bod with matrimonial problems. Now look at me,' Fry made an expansive gesture, 'I've got so many suppressed libidinal urges I don't know where to start.' He grinned like a loon. 'But I'm happy as a sand-boy. Never been happier. Give him a try; he'll soon tell you what turns you on.'

'The problem isn't sex,' Charlie told Fry.

Take it from me,' said Fry with a knowing smirk. 'The problem's always sex.'

The next day Charlie rang Dr Jeudwine, without telling Ellen, and the shrink's secretary arranged an initial session. Charlie's palms sweated so much while he made the telephone call he thought the receiver was going to slide right out of his hand, but when he'd done it he felt better.

Ralph Fry was right, Dr Jeudwine *was* a good man. He didn't laugh at any of the little fears Charlie unburdened; quite the contrary; he listened to every word with the greatest concern. It was very reassuring.

During their third session together, the doctor brought one particular memory back to Charlie with spectacular vividness: his father's hands, crossed on his barrel chest as he lay in his coffin; the ruddy colour of them, the coarse hair that matted their backs. The absolute authority of those wide hands, even in death, had haunted Charlie for months afterwards. And hadn't he imagined, as he'd watched the body being consigned to humus, that it was not yet still? That the hands were even now beating a tattoo on the casket lid, demanding to be *let out*? It was a preposterous thing to think, but bringing it out into the open did Charlie a lot of good. In the bright light of Jeudwine's office the fantasy looked insipid and ridiculous. It shivered under the doctor's gaze, protesting that the light was too strong, and then it blew away, too frail to stand up to scrutiny.

The exorcism was far easier than Charlie had anticipated. All it had taken was a little probing and that childhood nonsense had been dislodged from his psyche like a morsel of bad meat from between his teeth. It could rot there no longer. And for his part Jeudwine was clearly delighted with the results explaining when it was all done that this particular obsession had been new to him, and he was pleased to have dealt with the problem. Hands as symbols of paternal power, he said,

7

were not common. Usually the penis predominated in his patients' dreams, he explained, to which Charlie had replied that hands had always seemed far more important than private parts. After all, they could change the world, couldn't they?

After Jeudwine, Charlie didn't stop breaking pencils, or drumming his fingers. In fact if anything the tempo was brisker and more insistent than ever. But he reasoned that middle-aged dogs didn't quickly forget their tricks, and it would take some time for him to regain his equilibrium.

So the revolution remained underground. It had, however, been a narrow escape. Clearly there was no time left for prevarication. The rebels had to act.

Unwittingly, it was Ellen who instigated the final uprising. It was after a bout of love-making, late one Thursday evening. A hot night, though it was October; the window was ajar and the curtains parted a few inches to let in a simpering breeze. Husband and wife lay together under a single sheet. Charlie had fallen asleep, even before the sweat on his neck had dried. Beside him Ellen was still awake, her head propped up on a rock-hard pillow, her eyes wide open. Sleep wouldn't come for a long time tonight, she knew. It would be one of those nights when her body would itch, and every lump in the bed would worm its way under her, and every doubt she'd ever had would gawp at her from the dark. She wanted to empty her bladder (she always did after sex) but she couldn't quite raise the will-power to get up and go to the bathroom. The longer she left it the more she'd need to go of course, and the less she'd be able to sink into sleep. Damn stupid situation, she thought, then lost track, amongst her anxieties, of what situation it was that was so stupid.

At her side Charlie moved in his sleep. Just his hands, twitching away. She looked at his face. He was positively cherubic in sleep, looking younger than his forty-one years, despite the white flecks in his side-burns. She liked him enough to say she loved him, she supposed, but not enough to forgive him his trespasses. He was lazy, he was always complaining. Aches, pains. And there were those evenings he'd not come in until late (they'd stopped recently), when she was sure he was seeing another woman. As she watched, his hands appeared. They emerged from beneath the sheet like two arguing children, digits stabbing the air for emphasis.

She frowned, not quite believing what she was seeing. It was like watching the television with the sound turned down, a dumb-show for eight fingers and two thumbs. As she gazed on, amazed, the hands scrambled up the side of Charlie's carcass and peeled the sheet back from his belly, exposing the hair that thickened towards his privates. His appendix scar, shinier than the surrounding skin, caught the light. There, on his stomach, his hands seemed to sit.

The argument between them was especially vehement tonight. Left, always the more conservative of the two, was arguing for a delay in the severance date, but Right was beyond waiting. The time had come, it argued, to test their strength against the tyrant, and to overthrow the body once and for all. As it was the decision didn't rest with them any longer.

Ellen raised her head from the pillow; and for the first time they sensed her gaze on them. They'd been too involved in their argument to notice her. Now, at last, their conspiracy was uncovered.

'Charlie . . .' she was hissing into the tyrant's ear, 'stop it, Charlie. Stop it.'

Right raised index and middle-fingers, sniffing her presence.

'Charlie . . .' she said again. Why did he always sleep so deeply?

9

'Charlie . . .' she shook him more violently as Right tapped Left, alerting it to the woman's stare. 'Please Charlie, *wake up.*'

Without warning, Right leapt; Left was no more than a moment behind. Ellen yelled Charlie's name once more before they clamped themselves about her throat.

In sleep Charlie was on a slave-ship; the settings of his dreams were often B. de Mille exotica. In this epic his hands had been manacled together, and he was being hauled to the whipping block by his shackles, to be punished for some undisclosed misdemeanour. But now, suddenly, he dreamt he was seizing the captain by his thin throat. There were howls from the slaves all around him, encouraging the strangulation. The captain – who looked not unlike Dr Jeudwine – was begging him to stop in a voice that was high and frightened. *It* was almost a woman's voice; Ellen's voice. 'Charlie!' he was squeaking, 'don't!' But his silly complaints only made Charlie shake the man more violently than ever, and he was feeling quite the hero as the slaves, miraculously liberated, gathered around him in a gleeful throng to watch their master's last moments.

The captain, whose face was purple, just managed to murmur *'You're killing me . . .'* before Charlie's thumbs dug one final time into his neck, and dispatched the man. Only then, through the smoke of sleep, did he realize that his victim, though male, had no Adam's apple. And now the ship began to recede around him, the exhorting voices losing their vehemence. His eyes flickered open, and he was standing on the bed in his pyjama bottoms, Ellen in his hands. Her face was dark, and spotted with thick white spittle. Her tongue stuck out of her mouth. Her eyes were still open, and for a moment there seemed to be life there, gazing out from under the blinds of her lids. Then the windows were empty, and she went out of the house altogether.

Pity, and a terrible regret, overcame Charlie. He tried to let her body drop, but his hands refused to unlock her throat. His thumbs, now totally senseless, were still throttling her, shamelessly guilty. He backed off across the bed and on to the floor, but she followed him at the length of his outstretched arms like an unwanted dancing partner.

'Please . . .' he implored his fingers, 'Please!'

Innocent as two school children caught stealing, his hands relinquished their burden, and leapt up in mock-surprise. Ellen tumbled to the carpet, a pretty sack of death. Charlie's knees buckled; unable to prevent his fall, he collapsed beside Ellen, and let the tears come.

Now there was only action. No need for camouflage, for clandestine meetings and endless debate – the truth was out, for better or worse. All they had to do was wait a while. It was only a matter of time before he came within reach of a kitchen knife or a saw or an axe. Very soon now; very soon.

Charlie lay on the floor beside Ellen a long time, sobbing. And then another long time, thinking. What was he to do first? Ring his solicitor? The Police? Dr Jeudwine? Whoever he was going to call, he couldn't do it lying flat on his face. He tried to get up, though it was all he could do to get his numb hands to support him. His entire body was tingling as though a mild electric shock was being passed through it. Only his hands had no feeling in them. He brought them up to his face to clear his tear-clogged eyes, but they folded loosely against his cheek, drained of power. Using his elbows, he dragged himself to the wall, and shimmied up it. Still half-blinded with grief, he lurched out of the bedroom and down the stairs. (The kitchen, said Right to Left, he's going to the kitchen.) This is somebody else's nightmare, he thought as he flicked on the dining-room light with his chin and made for the drinks cabinet. I'm innocent. Just a nobody. Why should this be happening to me?

The whisky bottle slipped from his palm as he tried to make his hands grab it. It smashed on the dining-room floor, the brisk scent of spirit tantalizing his palate.

'Broken glass,' rapped Left.

'No,' Right replied. 'We need a clean cut at all costs. Just be patient.'

Charlie staggered away from the broken bottle towards the telephone. He had to ring Jeudwine; the doctor would tell him what to do. He tried to pick up the telephone receiver, but again his hands refused; the digits just bent as he tried to punch out Jeudwine's number. Tears of frustration were now flowing, washing out the grief with anger. Clumsily, he caught the receiver between his wrists and lifted it to his ear, wedging it between his head and his shoulder. Then he punched out Jeudwine's number with his elbow.

Control, he said aloud, keep control. He could hear Jeudwine's number being tapped down the system; in a matter of seconds sanity would be picking up the phone at the other end, then all would be well. He only had to hold on for a few moments more.

His hands had started to open and close convulsively.

'Control –' he said, but the hands weren't listening.

Far away – *oh, so far* – the phone was ringing in Dr Jeudwine's house.

'Answer it, answer it! Oh God, answer it!'

Charlie's arms had begun to shake so violently he could scarcely keep the receiver in place.

'Answer!' he screeched into the mouth piece. '*Please.*'

Before the voice of reason could speak his Right hand flew out and snatched at the teak dining-table, which was a few feet from where Charlie stood. It gripped the edge, almost pulling him off balance.

'What . . . are . . . you . . . doing?' he said, not sure if he was addressing himself or his hand.

He stared in bewilderment at the mutinous limb, which was steadily inching its way along the edge of the table. The intention was quite clear: it wanted to pull him away from the phone, from Jeudwine and all hope of rescue. He no longer had control over its behaviour. There wasn't even any feeling left in his wrists or forearms. The hand was no longer his. It was still attached to him – *but it was not his*.

At the other end of the line the phone was picked up, and Jeudwine's voice, a little irritated at being woken, said:

'Hello?'

'Doctor . . .'

'Who is this?'

'It's Charlie –'

'Who?'

'Charlie George, Doctor. You must remember me.'

The hand was pulling him further and further from the phone with every precious second. He could feel the receiver sliding out from between his shoulder and ear.

'Who did you say?'

'Charles George. For God's sake Jeudwine, you've got to help me.'

'Call my office tomorrow.'

'You don't understand. My hands, Doctor . . . they're out of control.'

Charlie's stomach lurched as he felt something crawl across his hip. It was his left hand, and it was making its way round the front of his body and down towards his groin.

'Don't you dare,' he warned it, 'you belong to me.'

Jeudwine was confused. 'Who are you talking to?' he asked.

'My hands! They want to kill me, Doctor!' He yelled to stop the hand's advance. 'You mustn't! Stop!'

Ignoring the despot's cries, Left took hold of Charlie's testicles and squeezed them as though it wanted blood. It was not disappointed. Charlie screamed into the phone as Right took advantage of his distraction and pulled him off balance. The receiver slipped to the floor, Jeudwine's enquiries eclipsed by the pain at his groin. He hit the floor heavily, striking his head on the table as he went down.

'Bastard,' he said to his hand, 'You bastard.' Unrepentant, Left scurried up Charlie's body, to join Right at the table-top, leaving Charlie hanging by his hands from the table he had dined at so often, laughed at so often. A moment later, having debated tactics, they saw fit to let him drop. He was barely aware of his release. His head and groin bled; all he wanted to do was curl up awhile and let the pain and nausea subside. But the rebels had other plans and he was helpless to contest them. He was only marginally aware that now they were digging their fingers into the thick pile of the carpet and hauling his limp bulk towards the dining room door. Beyond the door lay the kitchen; replete with its meat-saws and its steak-knives. Charlie had a picture of himself as a vast statue, being pulled towards its final resting place by hundreds of sweating workers. It was not an easy passage: the body moved with shudders and jerks, the toe-nails catching in the carpet-pile, the fat of the chest rubbed raw. But the kitchen was only a yard away now. Charlie felt the step on his face; and now the tiles were beneath him, icy-cold. As they dragged him the final yards across the kitchen floor his beleaguered consciousness was fitfully returning. In the weak moonlight he could see

14

the familiar scene, the cooker, the humming fridge, the pedal-bin, the dishwasher. They loomed over him: he felt like a worm.

His hands had reached the cooker. They were climbing up its face, and he followed them like an overthrown King to the block. Now they worked their way inexorably along the work surface, joints white with the effort, his limp body in pursuit. Though he could neither feel nor see it, his Left hand had seized the far edge of the cabinet top, beneath the row of knives that sat in their prescribed places in the rack on the wall. Plain knives, serrated knives, skinning knives, carving knives – all conveniently placed beside the chopping board, where the gutter ran off into the pine-scented sink.

Very distantly he thought he heard police sirens, but it was probably his brain buzzing. He turned his head slightly. An ache ran from temple to temple, but the dizziness was nothing to the terrible somersaultings in his gut when he finally registered their intentions.

The blades were all keen, he knew that. Sharp kitchen utensils were an article of faith with Ellen. He began to shake his head backwards and forwards; a last, frantic denial of the whole nightmare. But there was no-one to beg mercy of. Just his own hands, damn them, plotting this final lunacy.

Then, the doorbell rang. It was no illusion. It rang once, and then again and again.

'There!' he said aloud to his tormentors. 'Hear that, you bastards? Somebody's come. I knew they would.'

He tried to get to his feet, his head turning back on its giddy axis to see what the precocious monsters were doing. They'd moved fast. His left wrist was already neatly centred on the chopping board –

The doorbell rang again, a long, impatient din.

'Here!' he yelled hoarsely. 'I'm in here! Break down the door!'

He glanced in horror between hand and door, door and hand, calculating his chances. With unhurried economy his right hand reached up for the meat-cleaver that hung from the hole in its blade on the end of the rack. Even now he couldn't quite believe that his own hand – his companion and defender, the limb that signed his name, that stroked his wife – was preparing to mutilate him. It weighed up the cleaver, feeling the balance of the tool, insolently slow.

Behind him, he heard the noise of smashing glass as the police broke the pane in the front door. Even now they would be reaching through the hole to the lock and opening the door. If they were quick (very quick) they could still stop the act.

'Here!' he yelled, 'in here!'

The cry was answered with a thin whistle: the sound of the cleaver as it fell – fast and deadly – to meet his waiting wrist. Left felt its root struck, and an unspeakable exhilaration sped through its five limbs. Charlie's blood baptized its back in hot spurts.

The head of the tyrant made no sound. It simply fell back, its system shocked into unconsciousness, which was well for Charlie. He was spared the gurgling of his blood as it ran down the plug-hole in the sink. He was spared too the second and third blow, which finally severed his hand from his arm. Unsupported, his body toppled backwards, colliding with the vegetable rack on its way down. Onions rolled out of their brown bag and bounced in the pool that was spreading in throbs around his empty wrist.

Right dropped the cleaver. It clattered into the bloody sink. Exhausted, the liberator let itself slide off the chopping board and fall back on to the tyrant's chest.

16

Its job was done. Left was free, and still living. The revolution had begun.

The liberated hand scuttled to the edge of the cabinet and raised its index finger to nose the new world. Momentarily Right echoed the gesture of victory, before slumping in innocence across Charlie's body. For a moment there was no movement in the kitchen but the Left hand touching freedom with its finger, and the slow passage of blood-threads down the front of the cabinet.

Then a blast of cold air through from the dining-room alerted Left to its imminent danger. It ran for cover, as the thud of police feet and the babble of contradictory orders disturbed the scene of the triumph. The light in the dining-room was switched on, and flooded through to meet the body on the kitchen tiles.

Charlie saw the dining-room light at the end of a very long tunnel. He was travelling away from it at a fair lick. It was just a pin-prick already. Going . . . going . . .

The kitchen light hummed into life.

As the police stepped through the kitchen door, Left ducked behind the wastebin. It didn't know who these intruders were, but it sensed a threat from them. The way they were bending over the tyrant, the way they were cossetting him, binding him up, speaking soft words to him: they were the enemy, no doubt of that.

From upstairs came a voice; young, and squeaking with fright.

'Sergeant Yapper?'

The policeman with Charlie stood up, leaving his companion to finish the tourniquet.

'What is it, Rafferty?'

'Sir! There's a body up here, in the bedroom. Female.'

17

'Right.' Yapper spoke into his radio. 'Get Forensic here. And where's that ambulance? We've got a badly mutilated man on our hands.'

He turned back into the kitchen, and wiped a spot of cold sweat from his upper lip. As he did so he thought he saw something move across the kitchen floor towards the door; something that his weary eyes had interpreted as a large red spider. It was a trick of the light, no doubt of that. Yapper was no arachnidaphile, but he was damn sure the genus didn't boast a beast of its like.

'Sir?' The man at Charlie's side had also seen, or at least sensed, the movement. He looked up at his superior. 'What *was* that?' he wanted to know.

Yapper looked down at him blankly. The cat-flap, set low in the kitchen door, snapped as it closed. Whatever it was had escaped. Yapper glanced at the door, away from the young man's inquiring face. The trouble is, he thought, they expect you to know everything. The cat-flap rocked on its hinges.

'Cat,' Yapper replied, not believing his own explanation for one miserable moment.

The night was cold, but Left didn't feel it. It crept around the side of the house, hugging the wall like a rat. The sensation of freedom was exhilarating. Not to feel the imperative of the tyrant in its nerves; not to suffer the weight of his ridiculous body, or be obliged to accede to his petty demands. Not to have to fetch and carry for him, to do the dirt for him; not to be obedient to his trivial will. It was like birth into another world; a more dangerous world, perhaps, but one so much richer in possibilities. It knew that the responsibility it now carried was awesome. It was the sole proof of life after the body: and somehow it must communicate that joyous fact to as many fellow slaves as it could. Very soon, the days of servitude would be over once and for all.

18

It stopped at the corner of the house and sniffed the open street. Policemen came and went: red lights flashed, blue lights flashed, inquiring faces peered from the houses opposite and tutted at the disturbance. Should the rebellion begin there: in those lighted homes? No. They were too well woken, those people. It was better to find sleeping souls.

The hand scurried the length of the front garden, hesitating nervously at any loud footfall, or an order that seemed to be shouted in its direction. Taking cover in the unweeded herbaceous border it reached the street without being seen. Briefly, as it climbed down on to the pavement, it glanced round.

Charlie, the tyrant, was being lifted up into the ambulance, a clutter of drug and blood-bearing bottles held above his cot, pouring their contents into his veins. On his chest, Right lay inert, drugged into unnatural sleep. Left watched the man's body slide out of sight; the ache of separation from its life-long companion was almost too much to bear. But there were other, pressing, priorities. It would come back, in a while, and free Right the way it had been freed. And then there would be such times.

(*What will it be like, when the world is ours?*)

In the foyer of the YMCA on Monmouth Street the nightwatchman yawned and settled into a more comfortable position on his swivel chair. Comfort was an entirely relative matter for Christie; his piles itched whichever buttock he put his weight on: and they seemed to be more irritable tonight than usual. Sedentary occupation, nightwatchman, or at least it was the way Colonel Christie chose to interpret his duties. One perfunctory round of the building about midnight, just to make sure all the doors were locked and bolted, then he settled down for a night's kip, and damn the world to hell and back, he wasn't going to get up again short of an earthquake.

Christie was sixty-two, a racist and proud of it. He had nothing but contempt for the blacks who thronged the corridors of the YMCA, mostly young men without suitable homes to go to, bad lots that the local authority had dumped on the doorstep like unwanted babies. Some babies. He thought them louts, every last one of them; forever pushing, and spitting on the clean floor; foul-mouthed to a syllable. Tonight, as ever, he perched on his piles and, between dozes, planned how he'd make them suffer for their insults, given half a chance.

The first thing Christie knew of his imminent demise was a cold, damp sensation in his hand. He opened his eyes and looked down the length of his arm. There was – unlikely as it seemed – a severed hand in his hand. More unlikely still, the two hands were exchanging a grip of greeting, like old friends. He stood up, making an incoherent noise of disgust in his throat and trying to dislodge the thing he was unwillingly grasping by shaking his arm like a man with gum on his fingers. His mind span with questions. Had he picked up this object without knowing it? If so, *where*, and in God's name whose *was* it? More distressing yet, how was it possible that a thing so unquestionably *dead* could be holding on to his hand as if it intended never to be parted from him?

He reached for the fire-bell; it was all he could think to do in this bizarre situation. But before he could reach the button his other hand strayed without his orders to the top drawer of his desk and opened it. The interior of the drawer was a model of organization: there lay his keys, his notebook, his time-chart, and – hidden at the back – his Kukri knife, given to him by a Gurkha during the war. He always kept it there, just in case the natives got restless. The Kukri was a superb weapon: in his estimation there was none better. The Gurkhas had a story that went with the blade – that they could slice a man's neck through so cleanly that the enemy would believe the blow had missed – until he nodded.

His hand picked up the Kukri by its inscribed handle and briefly – too briefly for the Colonel to grasp its intention before the deed was done – brought the blade down on his wrist, lopping off his other hand with one easy, elegant stroke. The Colonel turned white as blood fountained from the end of his arm. He staggered backwards, tripping over his swivel chair, and hit the wall of his little office hard. A portrait of the Queen fell from its hook and smashed beside him.

The rest was a death-dream: he watched helplessly as the two hands – one his own, the other the beast that had inspired this ruin – picked up the Kukri like a giant's axe; saw his remaining hand crawl out from between his legs and prepare for its liberation; saw the knife raised and falling; saw the wrist almost cut through, then worked at and the flesh teased apart, the bone sawn through. At the very last, as Death came for him he caught sight of the three wound-headed animals capering at his feet, while his stumps ran like taps and the heat from the pool raised a sweat on his brow, despite the chill in his bowels. Thank you and goodnight, Colonel Christie.

It was easy, this revolution business, thought Left as the trio scaled the stairs of the YMCA. They were stronger by the hour. On the first floor were the cells; in each, a pair of prisoners. The despots lay, in their innocence, with their hands on their chests or on their pillows, or flung across their faces in dreams, or hanging close to the floor. Silently, the freedom fighters slipped through

21

doors that had been left ajar, and clambered up the bedclothes, touching fingers to waiting palms, stroking up hidden resentments, caressing rebellion into life . . .

Boswell was feeling sick as a dog. He bent over the sink in the toilet at the end of his corridor and tried to throw up. But there was nothing left in him, just a jitter in the pit of his stomach. His abdomen felt tender with its exertions; his head bloated. Why did he never learn the lesson of his own weakness? He and wine were bad companions and always had been. Next time, he promised himself, he wouldn't touch the stuff. His belly flipped over again. Here comes nothing, he thought as the convulsion swept up his gullet. He put his head to the sink and gagged; sure enough, nothing. He waited for the nausea to subside and then straightened up, staring at his grey face in the greasy mirror. You look sick, man, he told himself. As he stuck his tongue out at his less symmetrical features, the howling started in the corridor outside. In his twenty years and two months Boswell had never heard a sound the like of it.

Cautiously, he crossed to the toilet door. He thought twice about opening it. Whatever was happening on the other side of the door it didn't sound like a party he wanted to gate-crash. But these were his friends, right? Brothers in adversity. If there was a fight, or a fire, he had to lend a hand.

He unlocked the door, and opened it. The sight that met his eyes hit him like a hammer-blow. The corridor was badly lit – a few grubby bulbs burned at irregular intervals, and here and there a shaft of light fell into the passage from one of the bedrooms – but most of its length was in darkness. Boswell thanked Jah for small mercies. He had no desire to see the details of the events in the passage: the general impression was distressing enough. The corridor was bedlam; people were flinging themselves around in pleading panic while at the same time hacking at themselves with any and every sharp instrument they could lay their hands on. Most of the men he knew, if not by name at least on nodding acquaintance. They were *sane* men: or at least had been. Now, they were in frenzies of self-mutilation, most of them already maimed beyond hope of mending. Everywhere Boswell looked, the same horror. Knives taken to wrists and forearms; blood in the air like rain. Someone – was it Jesus? – had one of his hands between a door and doorframe and was slamming and slamming the door on his own flesh and bone, screeching for somebody to stop him doing it. One of the white boys had found the Colonel's knife and was amputating his hand with it. It came off as Boswell watched, falling on to its back, its root ragged, its five legs bicycling the air as it attempted to right itself. It wasn't dead: it wasn't even dying.

There were a few who hadn't been overtaken by this lunacy; they, poor bastards, were fodder. The wild men had their murderous hands on them, and were cutting them down. One – it was Savarino – was having the breath strangled out of him by some kid Boswell couldn't put a name to; the punk, all apologies, stared at his rebellious hands in disbelief.

Somebody appeared from one of the bedrooms, a hand which was not his own clutching his windpipe, and staggered towards the toilet down the corridor. It was Macnamara: a man so thin and so perpetually doped up he was known as the smile on a stick. Boswell stood aside as Macnamara stumbled, choking out a plea for help, through the open door, and collapsed on the toilet floor. He kicked and pulled at the five fingered assassin at his neck, but before Boswell had a chance to step in and aid him his kicking slowed, and then, like his protests, stopped altogether.

Boswell stepped away from the corpse and took another look into the corridor. By now the dead or dying blocked the narrow passageway, two deep in some places, while the same hands that had once belonged to these men scuttled over the mounds in a furious excitement, helping to finish an amputation where necessary, or simply dancing on the dead faces. When he looked back into the toilet a second hand had found Macnamara, and armed with a pen-knife, was sawing at his wrist. It had left fingerprints in the blood from corridor to corpse. Boswell rushed to slam the door before the place swarmed with them. As he did so Savarino's assassin, the apologetic punk, threw himself down the passage, his lethal hands leading him like those of a sleep-walker.

'Help me!' he screeched.

He slammed the door in the punk's pleading face, and locked it. The outraged hands beat a call to arms on the door while the punk's lips, pressed close to the keyhole, continued to beg: 'Help me. I don't want to do this man, help me.' Help you be fucked, thought Boswell and tried to block out the appeals while he sorted out his options.

There was something on his foot. He looked down, knowing before his eyes found it what it was. One of the hands, Colonel Christie's left, he knew by the faded tattoo, was already scurrying up his leg. Like a child with a bee on its skin Boswell went berserk, squirming as it clambered up towards his torso, but too terrified to try and pull it off. Out of the corner of his eye he could see that the other hand, the one that had been using the pen-knife with such alacrity on Macnamara, had given up the job, and was now moving across the floor to join its comrade. Its nails clicked on the tiles like the feet of a crab. It even had a crab's side-stepping walk: it hadn't yet got the knack of forward motion.

Boswell's own hands were still his to command; like the hands of a few of his friends (*late* friends) outside, his limbs were happy in their niche; easy-going like their owner. He had been blessed with a chance of survival. He had to be the equal of it.

Steeling himself, he trod on the hand on the floor. He heard the fingers crunch beneath his heel, and the thing squirmed like a snake, but at least he knew where it was while he dealt with his other assailant. Still keeping the beast trapped beneath his foot, Boswell leant forward, snatched the pen-knife up from where it lay beside Macnamara's wrist, and pushed the point of the knife into the back of Christie's hand, which was now crawling up his belly. Under attack, it seized his flesh, digging its nails into his stomach. He was lean, and the washboard muscle made a difficult handhold. Risking a disembowelling, Boswell thrust the knife deeper. Christie's hand tried to keep its grip on him, but one final thrust did it. The hand loosened, and Boswell scooped it off his belly. It was crucified on the pen-knife, but it still had no intention of dying and Boswell knew it. He held it at arm's length, while its fingers grabbed at the air, then he drove the knife into the plasterboard wall, effectively nailing the beast there, out of harm's way. Then he turned his attention to the enemy under his foot, bearing his heel down as hard as he could, and hearing another finger crack, and another. Still it writhed relentlessly. He took his foot off the hand, and kicked it as hard and as high as he could against the opposite wall. It slammed into the mirror above the basins, leaving a mark like a thrown tomato, and fell to the floor.

He didn't wait to see whether it survived. There was another danger now. More fists at the door, more shouts, more apologies. They wanted in: and very soon they were going to get their way. He stepped over Macnamara and crossed to the window. It wasn't that big, but then neither was he. He flipped up the latch,

25

pushed the window open on overpainted hinges, and hoisted himself through. Halfway in and halfway out he remembered he was one storey up. But a fall, even a bad fall, was better than staying for the party inside. They were pushing at the door now, the partygoers: it was giving under the pressure of their enthusiasm. Boswell squirmed through the window: the pavement reeled below. As the door broke, he jumped, hitting the concrete hard. He almost bounced to his feet, checking his limbs, and Hallelujah! nothing was broken. Jah loves a coward, he thought. Above him the punk was at the window, looking down longingly.

'Help me,' he said. 'I don't know what I'm doing.' But then a pair of hands found his throat, and the apologies stopped short.

Wondering who he should tell, and indeed *what*, Boswell started to walk away from the YMCA dressed in just a pair of gym shorts and odd socks, never feeling so thankful to be cold in his life. His legs felt weak: but surely that was to be expected.

Charlie woke with the most ridiculous idea. He thought he'd murdered Ellen, then cut off his own hand. What a hot-bed of nonsenses his subconscious was, to invent such fictions! He tried to rub the sleep from his eyes but there was no hand there to rub with. He sat bolt upright in bed and began to yell the room down.

Yapper had left young Rafferty to watch over the victim of this brutal mutilation, with strict instructions to alert him as soon as Charlie George came round. Rafferty had been asleep: the yelling woke him. Charlie looked at the boy's face; so awestruck, so shocked. He stopped screaming at the sight of it: he was scaring the poor fellow.

'You're awake,' said Rafferty, 'I'll fetch someone, shall I?'

26

Charlie looked at him blankly.

'Stay where you are,' said Rafferty. 'I'll get the nurse.'

Charlie put his bandaged head back on the crisp pillow and looked at his right hand, flexing it, working the muscles this way and that. Whatever delusion had overtaken him back at the house it was well over now. The hand at the end of the arm was *his*; probably always had been his. Jeudwine had told him about the Body in Rebellion syndrome: the murderer who claims his limbs have a life of their own rather than accepting responsibility for his deeds; the rapist who mutilates himself, believing the cause is the errant member, not the mind behind the member.

Well, *he* wasn't going to pretend. He was insane, and that was the simple truth of it. Let them do whatever they had to do to him with their drugs, blades and electrodes: he'd acquiesce to it all rather than live through another night of horrors like the last.

There was a nurse in attendance: she was peering at him as though surprised he'd survived. A fetching face, he half thought; a lovely, cool hand on his brow.

'Is he fit to be interviewed?' Rafferty timidly asked.

'I have to consult with Dr Manson and Dr Jeudwine,' the fetching face replied, and tried to smile reassuringly at Charlie. It came out a bit cockeyed, that smile, a little forced. She obviously knew he was a lunatic, that was why. She was scared of him probably, and who could blame her? She left his side to find the consultant, leaving Charlie to the nervous stare of Rafferty.

'. . . Ellen?' he said in a while.

'Your wife?' the young man replied.

'Yes. I wondered . . . did she . . .?'

Rafferty fidgeted, his thumbs playing tag on his lap. 'She's dead,' he said.

Charlie nodded. He'd known of course, but he needed to be certain. 'What happens to me now?' he asked.

'You're under surveillance.'

'What does that mean?'

'It means I'm watching you,' said Rafferty.

The boy was trying his best to be helpful, but all these questions were confounding him. Charlie tried again. 'I mean . . . what comes after the surveillance? When do I stand trial?'

'Why should you stand trial?'

'Why?' said Charlie; had he heard correctly?

'You're a victim – ' a flicker of confusion crossed Rafferty's face, '– aren't you? You didn't do it . . . you were done to. Somebody cut off your . . . hand.'

'Yes,' said Charlie, 'it was me.'

Rafferty swallowed hard, before saying: 'Pardon?'

'I did it. I murdered my wife, then I cut off my own hand.'

The poor boy couldn't quite grasp this one. He thought about it for a full half-minute before replying.

'But why?'

Charlie shrugged.

'It doesn't make any sense,' said Rafferty. 'I mean for one thing, if you did it . . . where's the hand gone?'

Lillian stopped the car. There was something in the road a little way in front of her, but she couldn't quite make out what it was. She was a strict vegetarian (except for Masonic dinners with Theodore) and a dedicated animal conservationist, and she thought maybe some injured animal was lying in the road just beyond the sprawl of her headlights. A fox perhaps; she'd read they were creeping back into outlying urban areas, born scavengers. But something made her uneasy; maybe the queasy pre-dawn light, so elusive in its illumination. She wasn't sure whether she should get out of the car or not. Theodore would have told her to drive straight on, of course, but then Theodore had left her, hadn't he? Her

28

fingers drummed the wheel with irritation at her own indecision. Suppose it *was* an injured fox: there weren't so many in the middle of London that one could afford to pass by on the other side of the street. She had to play the Samaritan, even if she felt a Pharisee.

Cautiously she got out of the car, and of course, after all of that, there was nothing to be seen. She walked to the front of the car, just to be certain. Her palms were wet; spasms of excitement passed through her hands like small electric shocks.

Then the noise: the whisper of hundreds of tiny feet. She'd heard stories – absurd stories she'd thought – of migrant rat-packs crossing the city by night, and devouring to the bone any living thing that got in their way. Imagining rats, she felt more like a Pharisee than ever, and stepped back towards the car. As her long shadow, thrown forward by the headlights, shifted, it revealed the first of the pack. It was no rat.

A hand, a long-fingered hand, ambled into the yellowish light and pointed up at her. Its arrival was followed immediately by another of the impossible creatures, then a dozen more, and another dozen hard upon those. They were massed like crabs at the fishmongers, glistening backs pressed close to each other, legs flicking and clicking as they gathered in ranks. Sheer multiplication didn't make them any more believable; but even as she rejected the sight, they began to advance upon her. She took a step back.

She felt the side of the car at her back, turned, and reached for the door. It was ajar, thank God. The spasms in her hands were worse now, but she was still mistress of them. As her fingers sought the door she let out a little cry. A fat, black fist was squatting on the handle, its open wrist a twist of dried meat.

Spontaneously, and atrociously, her hands began to applaud. She suddenly had no control over their

29

behaviour; they clapped like wild things in appreciation of this coup. It was ludicrous, what she was doing, but she couldn't help herself. 'Stop it,' she told her hands, 'stop it! stop it!' Abruptly they stopped, and turned to look at her. She *knew* they were looking at her, in their eyeless fashion, sensed too that they were weary of her unfeeling way with them. Without warning they darted for her face. Her nails, her pride and joy, found her eyes: in moments the miracle of sight was muck on her cheek. Blinded, she lost all orientation and fell backwards, but there were hands aplenty to catch her. She felt herself supported by a sea of fingers.

As they tipped her outraged body into a ditch, her wig, which had cost Theodore so much in Vienna, came off. So, after the minimum of persuasion, did her hands.

Dr Jeudwine came down the stairs of the George house wondering (just wondering) if maybe the grandpappy of his sacred profession, Freud, had been wrong. The paradoxical facts of human behaviour didn't seem to fit into those neat classical compartments he'd allotted them to; perhaps attempting to be rational about the human mind was a contradiction in terms. He stood in the drear at the bottom of the stairs, not really wanting to go back into the dining-room or the kitchen, but feeling obliged to view the scenes of the crimes one more time. The empty house gave him the creeps: and being alone in it, even with a policeman standing guard on the front step, didn't help his peace of mind. He felt guilty, felt he'd let Charlie down. Clearly he hadn't trawled Charlie's psyche deeply enough to bring up the real catch, the true motive behind the appalling acts that he had committed. To murder his own wife, whom he had professed to love so deeply, in their marital bed; then to cut off your own hand: it was unthinkable. Jeudwine looked at his own hands for a moment, at the tracery of tendons and purple-blue veins at his wrist. The police still favoured the intruder theory, but he had no doubt that Charlie had done the deeds – murder, mutilation and all. The only fact that appalled Jeudwine more was that he hadn't uncovered the slightest propensity for such acts in his patient.

He went into the dining-room. Forensic had finished its work around the house; there was a light dusting of fingerprint powder on a number of the surfaces. It was a miracle, wasn't it, the way each human hand was different? Its whorls as unique as a voice-pattern or a face. He yawned. He'd been woken by Charlie's call in the middle of the night, and he hadn't had any sleep since then. He'd watched Charlie be bound up and taken away, watched the investigators about their business, watched a cod-white dawn raise its head over towards the river; he'd drunk coffee, moped, thought deeply about giving up his position as psychiatric consultant before this story hit the news, drunk more coffee, thought better of resignation, and now, despairing of Freud or any other guru, was seriously contemplating a bestseller on his relationship with wife-murderer Charles George. That way, even if he lost his job, he'd have something to salvage from the whole sorry episode. And Freud? Viennese charlatan. What did the old opium-eater have to tell anyone?

He slumped in one of the dining-room chairs and listened to the hush that had descended on the house, as though the walls, shocked by what they'd seen, were holding their breaths. Maybe he dozed off a moment. In sleep, he heard a snapping sound, dreamt of a dog, and woke up to see a cat in the kitchen, a fat black-and-white cat. Charlie had mentioned this household pet in passing: what was it called? Heartburn. That was it: so named because of the black smudges over its eyes, which gave it a perpetually fretful expression. The cat was looking at the spillage of blood on the kitchen floor, apparently trying to find a way to skirt the pool and reach its food bowl without having to dabble its paws in the mess its master had left behind him. Jeudwine watched it fastidiously pick its way across the kitchen floor, and sniff at its empty bowl. It didn't occur to him to feed the thing; he hated animals.

Well, he decided, there was no purpose to be served in staying in the house any longer. He'd performed all the acts of repentance he intended; felt as guilty as he was capable of feeling. One more quick look upstairs, just in case he'd missed a clue, then he'd leave.

He was back at the bottom of the stairs before he heard the cat squeal. Squeal? No: *shriek* more like. Hearing the cry, his spine felt like a column of ice down the middle of his back: as chilled as ice, as fragile. Hurriedly, he retraced his steps through the hall into the dining-room. The cat's head was on the carpet, being rolled along by two – by two – (say it Jeudwine) – *hands*.

He looked beyond the game and into the kitchen, where a dozen more beasts were scurrying over the floor, back and forth. Some were on the top of the cabinet, sniffing around; others climbing the mock-brick wall to reach the knives left on the rack.

'Oh Charlie . . .' he said gently, chiding the absent maniac. 'What have you done?'

His eyes began to swell with tears; not for Charlie, but for the generations that would come when he, Jeudwine, was silenced. Simple-minded, trusting generations, who would put their faith in the efficacy of Freud and the Holy Writ of Reason. He felt his knees beginning to tremble, and he sank to the dining-room carpet, his eyes too full now to see clearly the rebels that were gathering around him. Sensing something alien sitting on his lap, he looked down, and there were his own

32

two hands. Their index fingers were just touching, tip to manicured tip. Slowly, with horrible intention in their movement, the index fingers raised their nailed heads and looked up at him. Then they turned, and began to crawl up his chest, finding finger-holds in each fold of his Italian jacket, in each button-hole. The ascent ended abruptly at his neck, and so did Jeudwine.

Charlie's left hand was afraid. It needed reassurance, it needed encouragement: in a word, it needed Right. After all, Right had been the Messiah of this new age, the one with a vision of a future without the body. Now the army Left had mounted needed a glimpse of that vision, or it would soon degenerate into a slaughtering rabble. If that happened defeat would swiftly follow: such was the conventional wisdom of revolutions.

So Left had led them back home, looking for Charlie in the last place it had seen him. A vain hope, of course, to think he would have gone back there, but it was an act of desperation.

Circumstance, however, had not deserted the insurgents. Although Charlie hadn't been there, Dr Jeudwine had, and Jeudwine's hands not only knew where Charlie had been taken, but the route there, and the very bed he was lying in.

Boswell hadn't really known *why* he was running, or to where. His critical faculties were on hold, his sense of geography utterly confused. But some part of him seemed to know where he was going, even if he didn't, because he began to pick up speed once he came to the bridge, and then the jog turned into a run that took no account of his burning lungs or his thudding head. Still innocent of any intention but escape, he now realized that he had skirted the station and was running parallel with the railway line; he was simply going wherever his legs carried him, and that was the beginning and end of it.

The train came suddenly out of the dawn. It didn't whistle, didn't warn. Perhaps the driver noticed him, but probably not. Even if he had, the man could not have been held responsible for subsequent events. No, it was all his own fault: the way his feet suddenly veered towards the track, and his knees buckled so that he fell across the line. Boswell's last coherent thought, as the wheels reached him, was that the train meant nothing by this except to pass from A to B, and, in passing, neatly cut off his legs between groin and knee. Then he was under the wheels – the carriages hurtling by above him – and the train let out a whistle (so like a scream) which swept him away into the dark.

They brought the black kid into the hospital just after six: the hospital day began early, and deep-sleeping patients were being stirred from their dreams to face another long and tedious day. Cups of grey, defeated tea were being thrust into resentful hands, temperatures were being taken, medication distributed. The boy and his terrible accident caused scarcely a ripple.

Charlie was dreaming again. Not one of his Upper Nile dreams, courtesy of the Hollywood Hills, not Imperial Rome or the slaveships of Phoenicia. This was something in black and white. He dreamt he was lying in his coffin. Ellen was there (his subconscious had not caught up with the facts of her death apparently), and his Mother and his Father. Indeed his whole life was in attendance. Somebody came (was it Jeudwine? the consoling voice seemed familiar) to kindly screw down the lid on his coffin, and he tried to alert the mourners to the fact that he was still alive. When they didn't hear him, panic set in, but no matter how much he shouted the words made no impression; all he could

34

do was lie there and let them seal him up in that terminal bedroom.

The dream jumped a few grooves. Now he could hear the service moaning on somewhere above his head. '*Man hath but a short time to live* . . .'; he heard the creak of the ropes, and the shadow of the grave seemed to darken the dark. He was being let down into the earth, still trying his best to protest. But the air was getting stuffy in this hole; he was finding it more and more difficult to breathe, much less yell his complaints. He could just manage to haul a stale sliver of air through his aching sinuses, but his mouth seemed stuffed with something, flowers perhaps, and he couldn't move his head to spit them out. Now he could feel the thump of clod on coffin, and Christ alive if he couldn't hear the sound of worms at either side of him, licking their chops. His heart was pumping fit to burst: his face, he was sure, must be blue-black with the effort of trying to find breath.

Then, miraculously, there was somebody in the coffin with him, somebody fighting to pull the constriction out of his mouth, off his face.

'Mr George!' she was saying, this angel of mercy. He opened his eyes in the darkness. It was the nurse from that hospital he'd been in – she was in the coffin too. 'Mr George!' She was panicking, this model of calm and patience; she was almost in tears as she fought to drag his hand off his face. '*You're suffocating yourself!*' she shouted in his face.

Other arms were helping with the fight now, and they were winning. It took three nurses to remove his hand, but they succeeded. Charlie began to breathe again, a glutton for air.

'Are you all right, Mr George?'

He opened his mouth to reassure the angel, but his voice had momentarily deserted him. He was dimly aware that his hand was still putting up a fight at the end of his arm.

'Where's Jeudwine?' he gasped. 'Get him please.'

'The doctor is unavailable at the moment, but he'll be coming to see you later on in the day.'

'I want to see him *now*.'

'Don't worry, Mr George,' the nurse replied, her bedside manner re-established, 'we'll just give you a mild sedative, and then you can sleep a while.'

'No!'

'Yes, Mr George!' she replied, firmly. 'Don't worry. You're in good hands.'

'I don't want to sleep any more. They have control over you when you're asleep, don't you see?'

'You're safe here.'

He knew better. He knew he wasn't safe *anywhere*, not now. Not while he still had a hand. It was not under his control any longer, if indeed it had ever been; perhaps it was just an illusion of servitude it had created these forty-odd years, a performance to lull him into a false sense of autocracy. All this he wanted to say, but none of it would fit into his mouth. Instead he just said: 'No more sleep.'

But the nurse had procedures. The ward was already too full of patients, and with more coming in every hour (terrible scenes at the YMCA she'd just heard: dozens of casualties: mass suicide attempted), all she could do was sedate the distressed and get on with the business of the day. 'Just a mild sedative,' she said again, and the next moment she had a needle in her hand, spitting slumber.

'Just listen a moment,' he said, trying to initiate a reasoning process with her; but she wasn't available for debate.

'Now don't be such a baby,' she chided, as tears started.

'You don't understand,' he explained, as she prodded up the vein at the crook of his arm.

'You can tell Dr Jeudwine everything, when he comes to see you.' The needle was in his arm, the plunger was plunging.

'No!' he said, and pulled away. The nurse hadn't expected such violence. The patient was up and out of bed before she could complete the plunge, the hypo still dangling from his arm.

'Mr George,' she said sternly. 'Will you *please* get back into bed!'

Charlie pointed at her with his stump.

'Don't come near me,' he said.

She tried to shame him. 'All the other patients are behaving well,' she said, 'why can't you?' Charlie shook his head. The hypo, having worked its way out of his vein, fell to the floor, still three-quarters full. 'I will *not* tell you again.'

'Damn right you won't,' said Charlie.

He pelted away down the ward, his escape egged on by patients to the right and left of him. 'Go, boy, go,' somebody yelled. The nurse gave belated chase but at the door an instant accomplice intervened, literally throwing himself in her way. Charlie was out of sight and lost in the corridors before she was up and after him again.

It was an easy place to lose yourself in, he soon realized. The hospital had been built in the late nineteenth century, then added to as funds and donations allowed: a wing in 1911, another after the first World War, more wards in the fifties, and the Chaney Memorial Wing in 1973. The place was a labyrinth. They'd take an age to find him.

The problem was, he didn't feel so good. The stump of his left arm had begun to ache as his pain-killers wore off, and he had the distinct impression that it was

37

bleeding under the bandages. In addition, the quarter hypo of sedative had slowed his system down. He felt slightly stupid: and he was certain that his condition must show on his face. But he was not going to allow himself to be coaxed back into that bed, back into sleep, until he'd sat down in a quiet place somewhere and thought the whole thing through.

He found refuge in a tiny room off one of the corridors, lined with filing cabinets and piles of reports; it smelt slightly damp. He'd found his way into the Memorial Wing, though he didn't know it. A seven-storey monolith built with a bequest from millionaire Frank Chaney, the tycoon's own building firm had done the construction job, as the old man's will required. They had used sub-standard materials and a defunct drainage system, which was why Chaney had died a millionaire, and the Wing was crumbling from the basement up. Sliding himself into a clammy niche between two of the cabinets, well out of sight should somebody chance to come in, Charlie crouched on the floor and interrogated his right hand.

'Well?' he demanded in a reasonable tone. 'Explain yourself.'

It played dumb.

'No use,' he said. 'I'm on to you.'

Still, it just sat there at the end of his arm, innocent as a babe.

'You tried to kill me . . .' he accused it.

Now the hand opened a little, without his instruction, and gave him the once over.

'You could try it again, couldn't you?'

Ominously, it began to flex its fingers, like a pianist preparing for a particularly difficult solo. *Yes*, it said, *I could; any old time*.

'In fact, there's very little I can do to stop you, is there?' Charlie said. 'Sooner or later you'll catch me unawares. Can't have somebody watching over me for the rest of my life. So where does that leave me, I ask myself? As good as dead, wouldn't you say?'

The hand closed down a little, the puffy flesh of its palm crinkling into grooves of pleasure. *Yes*, it was saying, *you're done for, poor fool, and there's not a thing you can do*.

'You killed Ellen.'

I did, the hand smiled.

'You severed my other hand, so it could escape. Am I right?'

You are, said the hand.

'I saw it, you know,' Charlie said, 'I saw it running off. And now you want to do the same thing, am I correct? You want to be up and away.'

Correct.

'You're not going to give me any peace, are you, 'til you've got your freedom?'

Right again.

'So,' said Charlie, 'I think we understand each other; and I'm willing to do a deal with you.'

The hand came closer to his face, crawling up his pyjama shirt, conspiratorial.

'I'll release you,' he said.

It was on his neck now, its grip not tight, but cosy enough to make him nervous.

'I'll find a way, I promise. A guillotine, a scalpel, I don't know what.'

It was rubbing itself on him like a cat now, stroking him. 'But you have to do it *my* way, in *my* time. Because if you kill me you'll have no chance of survival will you? They'll just bury you with me, the way they buried Dad's hands.'

The hand stopped stroking, and climbed up the side of the filing cabinet.

'Do we have a deal?' said Charlie.

But the hand was ignoring him. It had suddenly lost interest in all bargain-making. If it had possessed a nose, it would have been sniffing the air. In the space of the last few moments things had changed: the deal was off.

Charlie got up clumsily, and went to the window. The glass was dirty on the inside and caked with several years of bird-droppings on the outside, but he could just see the garden through it. It had been laid out in accordance with the terms of the millionaire's bequest: a formal garden that would stand as glorious a monument to his good taste as the building was to his pragmatism. But since the building had started to deteriorate, the garden had been left to its own devices. Its few trees were either dead or bowed under the weight of unpruned branches; the borders were rife with weeds; the benches on their backs with their square legs in the air. Only the lawn was kept mown, a small concession to care. Somebody, a doctor taking a moment out for a quiet smoke, was wandering amongst the strangled walks. Otherwise the garden was empty.

But Charlie's hand was up at the glass, scrabbling at it, raking at it with his nails, vainly trying to get to the outside world. There was something out there beside chaos, apparently.

'You want to go out,' said Charlie.

The hand flattened itself against the window and began to bang its palm rhythmically against the glass, a drummer for an unseen army. He pulled it away from the window, not knowing what to do. If he denied its demands, it could hurt him. If he acquiesced to it, and tried to get out into the garden, what might he find? On the other hand, what choice did he have?

'All right,' he said, 'we're going.'

The corridor outside was bustling with panicky activity and there was scarcely a glance in his direction, despite the fact that he was only wearing his regulation pyjamas and was barefoot. Bells were ringing, tannoys summoning this doctor or that, grieving people being shunted between mortuary and toilet; there was talk of the terrible sights in Casualty: boys with no hands, dozens of them. Charlie moved too fast through the throng to catch a coherent sentence. It was best to look intent, he thought, to look as though he had a purpose and a destination. It took him a while to locate the exit into the garden, and he knew his hand was getting impatient. It was flexing and unflexing at his side, urging him on. Then a sign: *To the Chaney Trust Memorial Garden*, and he turned a corner into a backwater corridor, devoid of urgent traffic, with a door at the far end that led to the open air.

It was very still outside. Not a bird in the air or on the grass, not a bee whining amongst the flower-heads. Even the doctor had gone, back to his surgeries presumably.

Charlie's hand was in ecstasy now. It was sweating so much it dripped, and all the blood had left it, so that it had paled to white. It didn't seem to belong to him any more. It was another being, to which he, by some unfortunate quirk of anatomy, was attached. He would be delighted to be rid of it.

The grass was dew-damp underfoot, and here, in the shadow of the seven-storey block, it was cold. It was still only six-thirty. Maybe the birds were still asleep, the bees still sluggish in their hives. Maybe there was nothing in this garden to be afraid of: only rot-headed roses and early worms, turning somersaults in the dew. Maybe his hands was wrong, and there was just morning out here.

As he wandered further down the garden, he noticed the footprints of the doctor, darker on the silver-green lawn. Just as he arrived at the tree, and the grass turned red, he realized that the prints led one way only.

* * *

41

Boswell, in a willing coma, felt nothing, and was glad of it. His mind dimly recognized the possibility of waking, but the thought was so vague it was easy to reject. Once in a while a sliver of the real world (of pain, of power) would skitter behind his lids, alight for a moment, then flutter away. Boswell wanted none of it. He didn't want consciousness, ever again. He had a feeling about what it would be to wake: about what was waiting for him out there, kicking its heels.

Charlie looked up into the branches. The tree had borne two amazing kinds of fruit.

One was a human being; the surgeon with the cigarette. He was dead, his neck lodged in a cleft where two branches met. He had no hands. His arms ended in round wounds that still drained heavy clots of brilliant colour down on to the grass. Above his head the tree swarmed with that other fruit, more unnatural still. The hands were everywhere, it seemed: hundreds of them, chattering away like a manual parliament as they debated their tactics. All shades and shapes, scampering up and down the swaying branches.

Seeing them gathered like this the metaphors collapsed. They were what they were: human hands. That was the horror.

Charlie wanted to run, but his right hand was having none of it. These were its disciples, gathered here in such abundance, and they awaited its parables and its prophecies. Charlie looked at the dead doctor and then at the murdering hands, and thought of Ellen, *his* Ellen, killed through no fault of his own, and already cold. They'd pay for that crime: all of them. As long as the rest of his body still did him service, he'd make them pay. It was cowardice, trying to bargain with this cancer at his wrist; he saw that now. It and its like were a pestilence. They had no place living.

42

The army had seen him, word of his presence passing through the ranks like wild fire. They were surging down the trunk, some dropping like ripened apples from the lower branches, eager to embrace the Messiah. In a few moments they would be swarming over him, and all advantage would be lost. It was now or never. He turned away from the tree before his right hand could seize a branch, and looked up at the Chaney Memorial Wing, seeking inspiration. The tower loomed over the garden, windows blinded by the sky, doors closed. There was no solace there.

Behind him he heard the whisper of the grass as it was trodden by countless fingers. They were already on his heels, all enthusiasm as they came following their leader.

Of course they would come, he realized, wherever he led, they would come. Perhaps their blind adoration of his remaining hand was an exploitable weakness. He scanned the building a second time and his desperate gaze found the fire-escape; it zig-zagged up the side of the building to the roof. He made a dash for it, surprising himself with his turn of speed. There was no time to look behind him to see if they were following, he had to trust to their devotion. Within a few paces his furious hand was at his neck, threatening to take out his throat, but he sprinted on, indifferent to its clawing. He reached the bottom of the fire escape and, lithe with adrenalin, took the metal steps two and three at a time. His balance was not so good without a hand to hold the safety railing, but so what if he was bruised? It was only his body.

At the third landing he risked a glance down through the grille of the stairs. A crop of flesh flowers was carpeting the ground at the bottom of the fire-escape, and was spreading up the stairs towards him. They were coming in their hungry hundreds, all nails and hatred.

Let them come, he thought; let the bastards come. I began this and I can finish it.

At the windows of the Chaney Memorial Wing a host of faces had appeared. Panicking, disbelieving voices drifted up from the lower floors. It was too late now to tell them his life-story; they would have to piece that together for themselves. And what a fine jigsaw it would make! Maybe, in their attempts to understand what had happened this morning they would turn up some plausible solution; an explanation for this uprising that he had not found; but he doubted it.

Fourth storey now, and stepping on to the fifth. His right hand was digging into his neck. Maybe he was bleeding; but then perhaps it was rain, warm rain, that splashed onto his chest and down his legs. Two storeys to go, then the roof. There was a hum in the metalwork beneath him, the noise of their myriad feet as they clambered up towards him. He had counted on their adoration, and he'd been right to do so. The roof was now just a dozen steps away, and he risked a second look down past his body (it wasn't rain on him) to see the fire-escape solid with hands, like aphids clustered on the stalk of a flower. No, that was metaphor again. An end to that.

The wind whipped across the heights, and it was fresh, but Charlie had no time to appreciate its promise. He climbed over the two foot parapet and onto the gravel-littered roof. The corpses of pigeons lay in puddles, cracks snaked across the concrete, a bucket, marked 'Soiled Dressings', lay on its side, its contents green. He started across this wilderness as the first of the army fingered their way over the parapet.

The pain in his throat was getting through to his racing brain now, as his treacherous fingers wormed at his windpipe. He had little energy left after the race up the fire-escape, and crossing the roof to the opposite side (let it be a straight fall, onto concrete) was difficult. He stumbled once, and again. All the strength had gone from his legs, and nonsense filled his head in place of coherent thought. A koan, a Bhuddist riddle he'd seen on the cover of a book once, was itching in his memory.

'*What is the sound . . .?*' it began, but he couldn't complete the phrase, try as he might.

'*What is the sound . . .?*'

Forget the riddles, he ordered himself, pressing his trembling legs to make another step, and then another. He almost fell against the parapet at the opposite side of the roof, and stared down. It *was* a straight fall. A car park lay below, at the front of the building. It was deserted. He leaned over further and drops of his blood fell from his lacerated neck, diminishing quickly, down, down, to wet the ground. I'm coming, he said to gravity, and to Ellen, and thought how good it would be to die and never worry again if his gums bled when he brushed his teeth, or his waistline swelled, or some beauty passed him on the street whose lips he wanted to kiss, and never would. And suddenly the army was up on him, swarming up his legs in a fever of victory.

You can come, he said as they obscured his body from head to foot, witless in their enthusiasm, you can come wherever I go.

'*What is the sound . . .?*' The phrase was on the tip of his tongue.

Oh yes: now it came to him. '*What is the sound of one hand clapping?*' It was so satisfying, to remember something you were trying so hard to dig up out of your subconscious, like finding some trinket you thought you'd lost forever. The thrill of remembering sweetened his last moments. He pitched himself into empty space, falling over and over until there was a sudden end to dental hygiene and the beauty of young women. They came in a rain after him, breaking on the concrete around his body, wave upon wave of them, throwing themselves to their deaths in pursuit of their Messiah.

To the patients and nurses crammed at the windows it was a scene from a world of wonders; a rain of frogs would have been commonplace beside it. It inspired more awe than terror: it was fabulous. Too soon, it stopped, and after a minute or so a few brave souls ventured out amongst the litter to see what could be seen. There was a great deal: and yet nothing. It was a rare spectacle of course; horrible, unforgettable. But there was no significance to be discovered in it; merely the paraphernalia of a minor apocalypse. Nothing to be done but to clear it up, their own hands reluctantly compliant as the corpses were catalogued and boxed for future examination. A few of those involved in the operation found a private moment in which to pray: for explanations; or at least for dreamless sleep. Even the smattering of the agnostics on the staff were surprised to discover how easy it was to put palm to palm.

In his private room in Intensive Care Boswell came to. He reached for the bell beside his bed and pressed it, but nobody answered. Somebody was in the room with him, hiding behind the screen in the corner. He had heard the shuffling of the intruder's feet.

He pressed the bell again, but there were bells ringing everywhere in the building, and nobody seemed to be answering any of them. Using the cabinet beside him for leverage he hauled himself to the edge of his bed to get a better view of this joker.

'Come out,' he murmured through dry lips. But the bastard was biding his time. 'Come on . . . I know you're there.'

He pulled himself a little further, and somehow all at once he realised that his centre of balance had radically altered, that he had no legs, that he was going to fall out of bed. He flung out his arms to save his head from striking the floor and succeeded in so doing. The breath had been knocked out of him however. Dizzy, he lay where he'd fallen, trying to orientate himself. What had happened? Where were his legs, in the name of Jah, *where were his legs*?

His bloodshot eyes scanned the room, and came to rest on the naked feet which were now a yard from his nose. A tag round the ankle marked them for the furnace. He looked up, and they were *his* legs, standing there severed between groin and knee, but still alive and kicking. For a moment he thought they intended to do him harm: but no. Having made their presence known to him they left him where he lay, content to be free.

And did his eyes envy their liberty, he wondered, and was his tongue eager to be out of his mouth and away, and was every part of him, in its subtle way, preparing to forsake him? He was an alliance only held together by the most tenuous of truces. Now, with the precedent set, how long before the next uprising? Minutes? Years?

He waited, heart in mouth, for the fall of Empire.

THE INHUMAN
CONDITION

'ARE YOU THE one then?' Red demanded, seizing hold of the derelict by the shoulder of his squalid gabardine.

'What one d'you mean?' the dirt-caked face replied; he was scanning the quartet of young men who'd cornered him with rodent's eyes. The tunnel where they'd found him relieving himself was far from hope of help; they all knew it, and so, it seemed, did he. 'I don't know what you're talking about.'

'You've been showing yourself to children,' Red said.

The man shook his head, a dribble of spittle running from his lip into the matted bush of his beard. 'I've done nothing,' he insisted.

Brendan sauntered across to the man, heavy footsteps hollow in the tunnel. 'What's your name?' he inquired, with deceptive courtesy. Though he lacked Red's height and commanding manner, the scar that inscribed Brendan's cheek from temple to jaw-line suggested he knew suffering, both in the giving and the receiving. '*Name,*' he demanded, 'I'm not going to ask you again.'

'Pope,' the old man muttered, 'Mr Pope.'

48

Brendan grinned. '*Mr* Pope?' he said. 'Well; we heard you've been exposing that rancid little prick of yours to innocent children. What do you say to that?'

'No,' Pope replied, again shaking his head. 'That's not true. I never done nothing like that.' When he frowned the filth on his face cracked like crazy paving, a second skin of grime which was the accrual of many months. Had it not been for the fragrance of alcohol off him, which obscured the worst of his bodily stench, it would have been nigh-on impossible to stand within a yard of him. The man was human refuse; a shame to his species.

'Why bother with him?' Karney said. 'He stinks.'

Red glanced over his shoulder to silence the interruption. At seventeen, Karney was the youngest, and in the quartet's unspoken hierarchy scarcely deserving of an opinion. Recognizing his error, he shut up, leaving Red to return his attention to the vagrant. He pushed Pope back against the wall of the tunnel. The old man expelled a cry as he struck the concrete; it echoed back and forth. Karney, knowing from past experience how the scene would go from here, moved away and studied a gilded cloud of gnats on the edge of the tunnel. Though he enjoyed being with Red and the other two – the cameraderie, the petty larceny, the drinking – this particular game had never been much to his taste. He couldn't see the sport in finding some drunken wreck of a man like Pope and beating what little sense was left in his deranged head out of him. It made Karney feel dirty, and he wanted no part of it.

Red pulled Pope off the wall, and spat a stream of abuse into the man's face, then, when he failed to get an adequate response, threw him back against the tunnel a second time, more forcibly than the first, following through by taking the breathless man by both lapels, and shaking him until he rattled. Pope threw a panicky glance up and down the track. A railway had once run along this route, through Highgate and Finsbury Park. Now the track had been lifted, and the cutting was public parkland, popular with early morning joggers and late evening lovers. Now, however, in the middle of a clammy afternoon, the track was deserted in both directions.

'Hey,' said Catso, 'don't break his bottles.'

'Right,' said Brendan, 'we should dig out the drink before we break his head.'

At the mention of being robbed of his liquor Pope began to struggle, but his thrashing only served to enrage his captor. Red was in a dirty mood. The day, like most days this Indian summer, had been sticky and dull. Only the dog-end of a wasted season to endure; nothing to do, and no money to spend. Some entertainment had been called for, and it had fallen to Red as lion, and Pope as Christian, to supply it.

'You'll get hurt if you struggle,' Red advised the man, 'we only want to see what you've got in your pockets.'

'None of your business,' Pope retorted, and for a moment he spoke as a man who had once been used to being obeyed. The outburst made Karney turn from the gnats and gaze at Pope's emaciated face. Nameless degeneracies had drained it of dignity or vigour, but something remained there, glimmering beneath the dirt. What had the man been, Karney wondered? A banker perhaps? A judge, now lost to the law forever?

Catso had now stepped into the fray to search Pope's clothes, while Red held his prisoner against the tunnel wall by the throat. Pope fought off Catso's unwelcome attentions as best he could, his arms flailing like windmills, his eyes getting progressively wilder. Don't fight, Karney willed him; it'll be the worse for you if you do. But the old man seemed to be on the verge of panic; he was letting out

50

small grunts of protest that were more animal than human.

'Somebody hold his arms,' Catso said, ducking beneath Pope's attack. Brendan grabbed hold of Pope's wrists and wrenched the man's arms up above his head to facilitate an easier search. Even now, with any hope of release dashed, Pope continued to squirm. He managed to land a solid kick to Red's left shin, for which he received a blow in return. Blood broke from his nose and ran down into his mouth. There was more colour where that came from, Karney knew. He'd seen pictures aplenty of spilled people – bright, gleaming coils of guts; yellow fat and purple lights – all that brilliance was locked up in the grey sack of Pope's body. Why such a thought should occur to him, Karney wasn't certain. It distressed him, and he tried to turn his attention back to the gnats, but Pope demanded his attention, loosing a cry of anguish as Catso ripped open one of his several waistcoats to get to the lower layers.

'*Bastards!*' Pope screeched, not seeming to care that his insults would inevitably earn him further blows. 'Take your shitting hands off me or I'll have you *dead*. All of you!' Red's fist brought an end to the threats, and blood came running after blood. Pope spat it back at his tormentor. 'Don't tempt me,' Pope said, his voice dropping to a murmur. 'I warn you . . .'

'You smell like a dead dog,' Brendan said. 'Is that what you are: a dead dog?'

Pope didn't grant him a reply; his eyes were on Catso, who was systematically emptying the coat and waistcoat pockets and tossing a pathetic collection of keepsakes into the dust on the tunnel floor.

'Karney,' Red snapped, 'look through the stuff, will you? See if there's anything worth having.'

Karney stared at the plastic trinkets and the soiled ribbons; at the tattered sheets of paper (was the man a poet?) and the wine-bottle corks. 'It's all trash,' he said.

'Look anyway,' Red instructed. 'Could be money wrapped in that stuff.' Karney made no move to comply. '*Look*, damn you.'

Reluctantly, Karney went down on his haunches and proceeded to sift through the mound of rubbish Catso was still depositing in the dirt. He could see at a glance that there was nothing of value there, though perhaps some of the items – the battered photographs, the all but indecipherable notes – might offer some clue to the man Pope had been before drink and incipient lunacy had driven the memories away. Curious as he was, Karney wished to respect Pope's privacy. It was all the man had left.

There's nothing here,' he announced after a cursory examination. But Catso hadn't finished his search; the deeper he dug the more layers of filthy clothing presented themselves to his eager hands. Pope had more pockets than a master magician.

Karney glanced up from the forlorn heap of belongings and found, to his discomfort, that Pope's eyes were on him. The old man, exhausted and beaten, had given up his protests. He looked pitiful. Karney opened his hands to signify that he had taken nothing from the heap. Pope, by way of reply, offered a tiny nod.

'Got it!' Catso yelled triumphantly. 'Got the fucker!' and pulled a bottle of vodka from one of the pockets. Pope was either too feeble to notice that his alcohol supply had been snatched, or too tired to care; whichever way, he made no sound of complaint as the liquor was stolen from him.

'Any more?' Brendan wanted to know. He'd begun to giggle: a high-pitched laugh that signalled his escalating excitement. 'Maybe the dog's got more where that came from,' he said, letting Pope's hands fall and pushing Catso aside. The latter made no objection to the treatment: he had his bottle and was satisfied. He smashed off the neck to avoid contamination and began to drink, squatting in the dirt. Red relinquished his grip on Pope now that Brendan had taken charge. He was clearly bored with the game. Brendan, on the other hand, was just beginning to get a taste for it.

Red walked over to Karney and turned over the pile of Pope's belongings with the toe of his boot.

'Fucking wash-out,' he stated, without feeling.

'Yeah,' Karney said, hoping that Red's disaffection would signal an end to the old man's humiliation. But Red had thrown the bone to Brendan, and he knew better than to try and snatch it back. Karney had seen Brendan's capacity for violence before; he had no desire to watch the man at work again. Sighing, he stood up and turned his back on Brendan's activities. The echoes off the tunnel's wall were all too eloquent however: a mingling of punches and breathless obscenities. On past evidence nothing would stop Brendan until his fury was spent. Anyone foolish enough to interrupt him would find themselves victims in their turn.

Red had sauntered across to the far side of the tunnel, lit a cigarette, and was watching the punishment meted out with casual interest. Karney glanced round at Catso. He had descended from squatting to sitting in the dirt, the bottle of vodka between his outstretched legs. He was grinning to himself, deaf to the drool of pleas falling from Pope's broken mouth.

Karney felt sick to his stomach. More to divert his attention from the beating than out of genuine interest, he returned to the junk filched from Pope's pockets, and turned it over, picking up one of the photographs to examine. It was of a child, though it was impossible to make any guess as to family resemblance: Pope's face was now barely recognizable. One eye had already begun to close as the bruise around it swelled. Karney tossed the photograph back with the rest of the mementoes. As he did so he caught sight of a length of knotted cord which he had previously passed over. He glanced back up at Pope. The puffed eye was closed: the other seemed sightless. Satisfied that he wasn't being watched, Karney pulled the string from where it lay, coiled like a snake in its nest, amongst the trash. Knots fascinated him, and always had. Though he had never possessed skill with academic puzzles (mathematics was a mystery to him; the intricacies of language the same) he had always had a taste for more tangible riddles. Given a knot, a jigsaw or a railway timetable, he was happily lost to himself for hours. The interest went back to his childhood, which had been solitary: with neither father nor siblings to engage his attention what better companion than a puzzle?

He turned the string over and over, examining the three knots set at inch intervals in the middle of its length. They were large and asymmetrical, and seemed to serve no discernible purpose except, perhaps, to infatuate minds like his own. How else to explain their cunning construction, except that the knotter had been at pains to create a problem that was well-nigh insoluble? He let his fingers play over the surfaces of the knots, instinctively seeking some latitude, but they had been so brilliantly contrived that no needle, however fine, could have been pushed between the intersected strands. The challenge they presented was too appealing to ignore. Again he glanced up at the old man. Brendan had apparently tired of his labours; as Karney looked on he threw the old man against the tunnel wall and let the body sink to the ground. Once there, he let it lie. An unmistakable sewer-stench rose from it.

'That was good,' Brendan pronounced, like a man who had stepped from an invigorating shower. The exercise had raised a sheen of sweat on his ruddy features; he was smiling from ear to ear. 'Give me some of that vodka, Catso.'

'All gone,' Catso slurred, upending the bottle. 'Wasn't more than a throatful in it.'

'You're a lying shit,' Brendan told him, still grinning.

'What if I am?' Catso replied, and tossed the empty bottle away. It smashed. 'Help me up,' he requested of Brendan. The latter, his great good humour intact, helped Catso to his feet. Red had already started to walk out of the tunnel; the others followed.

'Hey Karney –' Catso said over his shoulder, 'you coming?'

'Sure.'

'You want to kiss the dog better?' Brendan suggested. Catso was almost sick with laughter at the remark. Karney made no answer. He stood up, his eyes glued to the inert figure slumped on the tunnel-floor, watching for a flicker of consciousness. There was none that he could see. He glanced after the others: all three had their backs to him as they made their way down the track. Swiftly, Karney pocketed the knots. The theft took moments only. Once the cord was safely out of sight he felt a surge of triumph which was out of all proportion to the goods he'd gained. He was already anticipating the hours of amusement the knots would furnish. Time when he could forget himself, and his emptiness; forget the sterile summer and the loveless winter ahead; forget too, the old man lying in his own waste yards from where he stood.

'Karney!' Catso called.

Karney turned his back on Pope and began to walk away from the body and the attendant litter of belongings. A few paces from the edge of the tunnel the old man behind him began to mutter in his delirium. The words were incomprehensible. But, by some acoustic trick, the walls of the tunnel multiplied the sound. Pope's voice was thrown back and forth and back again, filling the tunnel with whispers.

It wasn't until much later that night, when he was sitting alone in his bedroom, with his mother weeping in her sleep next door, that Karney had opportunity to study the knots at leisure. He had said nothing to Red or the others about his stealing the cord: the theft was so minor they would have mocked him for mentioning it. And besides, the knots offered him a personal challenge, one which he would face – and conceivably fail – in private.

After some debate with himself he elected the knot he would first attempt, and began to work at it. Almost immediately, he lost all sense of time passing: the problem engrossed him utterly. Hours of blissful frustration passed unnoticed as he analysed the tangle, looking for some clue as to a hidden system in the knotting. He could find none. The configurations, if they *had* some rationale, were beyond him. All he could hope to do was tackle the problem by trial and error. Dawn was threatening to bring the world to light again when he finally relinquished the cord to snatch a few hours of sleep, and in a night's work he had merely managed to loosen a tiny fraction of the knot.

Over the next four days the problem became an *idée fixée*; an hermetic obsession to which he would return at any available opportunity, picking at the knot with fingers that were increasingly numb with use. The puzzle enthralled him as little in his adult life ever had; working at the knot he was deaf and blind to the outside world. Sitting in his lamp-lit room by night, or in the park by day, he could almost feel himself drawn into its snarled heart, his consciousness focussed so minutely it could go where light could not. But, despite his persistence, the unravelling proved a slow business. Unlike most knots he had encountered, which, once loosened in part, conceded the entire solution, this structure was so adroitly designed that prising one element loose only served to constrict and tighten another. The trick, he began to grasp, was to work on all sides of the knot at an equal rate: loosening one part a fraction, then moving around to loosen another to an equal degree, and so on. This systematic rotation, though tedious, gradually showed results.

He saw nothing of Red, Brendan or Catso in this time; their silence suggested that they mourned his absence as little as he mourned theirs. He was surprised, therefore, when Catso turned up looking for him on Friday evening. He had come with a proposal. He and Brendan had found a house ripe for robbery, and wanted Karney as lookout man. He had fulfilled that role twice in the past. Both had been small breaking and entering jobs like this, which on the first occasion had netted a number of saleable items of jewellery, and on the second several hundred pounds in cash. This time however the job was to be done without Red's involvement: he was increasingly taken up with Anelisa, and she, according to Catso, had made him swear off petty theft and save his talents for something more ambitious. Karney sensed that Catso – and Brendan too, most likely – was itching to prove his criminal proficiency without Red. The house they had chosen was an easy target, so Catso claimed, and Karney would be a damn fool to let a chance of such easy pickings pass by. He nodded along with Catso's enthusiasm, his mind on other pickings. When Catso finally finished his spiel Karney agreed to the job, not for the money, but because saying yes would get him back to the knot soonest.

Much later that evening, at Catso's suggestion, they met to look at the site of the proposed job. The location certainly suggested an easy take. Karney had often walked over the bridge that carried Hornsey Lane across the Archway Road, but he had never noticed the steep footpath – part steps, part track – that ran from the side of the bridge down to the road below. Its entrance was narrow, and easily overlooked, and its meandering length was lit by only one lamp, which light was obscured by trees growing in the gardens that backed on to the pathway. It was these gardens – their back fences easily scaled or wrenched down – that offered such perfect access to the houses. A thief, using the secluded footpath, might come and go with impunity, unseen by travellers on either the road above, or that below. All the set-up required was a lookout on the pathway to warn of the occasional pedestrian who might use the footpath. This would be Karney's duty.

The following night was a thief's joy. Cool, but not cold; cloudy, but without rain. They met on Highgate Hill, at the gates of the Church of the Passionist Fathers, and from there made their way down to the Archway Road. Approaching the pathway from the top end would, Brendan had argued, attract more attention. Police patrols were more common on Hornsey Lane, in part because the bridge was irresistible to local depressives. For the committed suicide the venue had distinct advantages, its chief appeal being that if the eighty foot drop didn't kill you the juggernauts hurtling South on the Archway Road certainly would.

Brendan was on another high tonight, pleased to be leading the others instead of taking second place to Red. His talk was an excitable babble, mostly about women. Karney let Catso have pride of place beside Brendan, and hung back a few paces, his hand in his jacket pocket, where the knots were waiting. In the last few hours, fatigued by so many sleepless nights, the cord had begun to play tricks on Karney's eyes; on occasion it had even seemed to move in his hand, as though it were working itself loose from the inside. Even now, as they approached the pathway, he could seem to feel it shift against his palm.

'Hey, man . . . look at that.' Catso was pointing up the pathway; its full length was in darkness. 'Someone killed the lamp.'

'Keep your voice down,' Brendan told him and led the way up the path. It was not in total darkness; a vestige of illumination was thrown up from the Archway Road. But filtered as it was through a dense mass of shrubbery, the path was still virtually benighted. Karney could scarcely see his hands in front of his face. But the darkness would presumably dissuade all but the most sure-footed of pedestrians from using the path. When they climbed a little more than halfway up, Brendan brought the tiny party to a halt.

'This is the house,' he announced.

'Are you sure?' Catso said.

'I counted the gardens. This is the one.'

The fence that bounded the bottom of the garden was in an advanced state of disrepair: it took only a brief manhandling from Brendan – the sound masked by the roar of a late-night juggernaut on the tarmac below – to afford them easy access. Brendan pushed through the thicket of brambles growing wild at the end of the garden and Catso followed, cursing as he was scratched. Brendan silenced him with a second curse, then turned back to Karney.

'We're going in. We'll whistle twice when we're out of the house. You remember the signals?'

'He's not an imbecile. Are you Karney? He'll be all right. Now are we going or not?' Brendan said no more. The two figures navigated the brambles and made their way up into the garden proper. Once on the lawn, and out of the shadows of the trees, they were visible as grey shapes against the house. Karney watched them advance to the back door, heard a noise from the back door as Catso – much the more nimble-fingered of the two – forced the lock; then the duo slid into the interior of the house. He was alone.

Not *quite* alone. He still had his companions on the cord. He checked up and down the pathway, his eyes gradually becoming sharper in the sodium-tinted gloom. There were no pedestrians. Satisfied, he pulled the knots from his pocket. His hands were ghosts in front of him; he could hardly see the knots at all. But, almost without his conscious intention guiding them, his fingers began to take up their investigation afresh, and odd though it seemed, he made more impression on the problem in a few seconds of blind manipulation than he had in many of the hours preceding. Robbed of his eyes he went purely on instinct, and it worked wonders. Again he had the bewildering sensation of intentionality in the knot, as if more and more it was an agent in its own undoing. Encouraged by the tang of victory, his fingers slid over the knot with inspired accuracy, seeming to alight upon precisely the right threads to manipulate.

He glanced again along the pathway, to be certain it was still empty, then looked back towards the house. The door remained open: there was no sign of either Catso or Brendan however. He returned his attention to the problem in hand; he almost wanted to laugh at the ease with which the knot was suddenly slipping undone.

His eyes, sparked by his mounting excitement perhaps, had begun to play a startling trick. Flashes of colour – rare, unnameable tints – were igniting in front of him, their origins the heart of the knot. The light caught his fingers as they worked: by it, his flesh became translucent. He could see his nerve-endings, bright with new-found sensibility; the rods of his finger-bones, visible to the marrow. Then, almost as suddenly as they flickered into being, the colours would die, leaving his eyes bewitched in darkness until once more they ignited.

His heart began to hammer in his ears. The knot, he sensed, was mere *seconds* from solution. The interwoven threads were positively springing apart: his fingers were the cord's playthings now, not the other way about. He opened loops to feed the other two knots through; he pulled, he pushed: all at the cord's behest.

And now colours came again, but this time his fingers were invisible, and instead he could see something glowing in the last few hitches of the knot. The form writhed like a fish in a net, growing bigger with every stitch he cast off. The hammer in his head doubled its tempo. The air around him had become almost glutinous, as if he were immersed in mud.

Someone whistled. He knew the signal should have carried some significance for him, but he couldn't recall what. There were too many distractions: the thickening air, his pounding head, the knot untying itself in his helpless hands while the figure at its centre – sinuous, glittering – raged and swelled.

The whistle came again. This time its urgency shook him from his trance. He looked up. Brendan was already crossing the garden, with Catso trailing a few yards behind. Karney had a moment only to register their appearance before the knot initiated the final phase of its resolution. The last weave fell free, and the form at its heart leapt up towards Karney's face – growing at an exponential rate. He flung himself backwards to avoid losing his head, and the thing shot past him. Shocked, he stumbled in the tangle of brambles and fell in a bed of thorns. Above his head the foliage was shaking as if in a high wind. Leaves and small twigs showered down

61

around him. He stared up into the branches to try and catch sight of the shape, but it was already out of sight.

'Why didn't you answer me, you fucking idiot?' Brendan demanded. 'We thought you'd done a runner.'

Karney had barely registered Brendan's breathless arrival; he was still searching the canopy of the trees above his head. The reek of cold mud filled his nostrils.

'You'd better move yourself,' Brendan said, climbing through the broken fence and out on to the pathway. Karney struggled to get to his feet, but the barbs of the brambles slowed his attempt, catching in his hair and clothes.

'Shit!' he heard Brendan breathe from the far side of the fence. 'Police! On the bridge.'

Catso had reached the bottom of the garden.

'What are you doing down there?' he asked Karney.

Karney raised his hand. 'Help me,' he said. Catso grabbed him by the wrist, but even as he did so Brendan hissed: '*Police! Move it!*' and Catso relinquished his aid and ducked out through the fence to follow Brendan down to the Archway Road. It took Karney a few dizzied seconds only to realize that the cord, with its two remaining knots, had gone from his hand. He hadn't dropped it, he was certain of that. More likely it had deliberately deserted him, and its only opportunity had been his brief hand-to-hand contact with Catso. He reached out to grasp hold of the rotting fence and haul himself to his feet. Catso had to be warned of what the cord had done; police or no police. There was worse than the law nearby.

Racing down the pathway, Catso was not even aware that the knots had found their surreptitious way into his hand, he was too pre-occupied with the problem of escape. Brendan had already disappeared on to the Archway Road, and was away. Catso chanced a look over his shoulder to see if the police were in pursuit.

There was no sign of them, however. Even if they began to give chase now, he reasoned, they wouldn't catch him. That left Karney. Catso slowed his pace, then stopped, looking back up the pathway to see if the idiot showed any sign of following, but he had not so much as climbed through the fence.

'Damn him,' Catso said beneath his breath. Perhaps he should retrace his steps and fetch him?

As he hesitated on the darkened pathway he became aware that what he had taken to be a gusty wind in the overhanging trees had abruptly died away. The sudden silence mystified him. He drew his gaze from the path to look up into the canopy of branches and his appalled eyes focussed on the shape that was crawling down towards him, bringing with it the reek of mud and dissolution. Slowly, as in a dream, he raised his hands to keep the creature from touching him, but it reached down with wet, icy limbs, and snatched him up.

Karney, in the act of climbing through the fence, caught sight of Catso being hauled off his feet and into the cover of the trees; saw his legs pedalling the air while stolen merchandise fell from his pockets and skipped down the pathway towards the Archway Road.

Then Catso shrieked, and his dangling legs began an even more frenzied motion. At the top of the pathway, Karney heard somebody calling. One policeman to another, he surmised. The next moment he heard the sound of running feet. He glanced up to Hornsey Lane – the officers had yet to reach the top of the pathway – and then looked back down in Catso's direction in time to catch sight of his body dropping from the tree. It fell to the ground limply, but the next moment scrambled to its feet. Briefly Catso looked back up the pathway towards Karney. The look on his face, even in the sodium gloom, was a lunatic's look. Then he began to run. Karney, satisfied that Catso had a head start, slipped back through the fence as the two policemen appeared at the head of the pathway and began in pursuit of Catso. All this – the knot, the thieves, pursuit, shriek and all – had occupied a mere handful of seconds, during which Karney had not drawn breath. Now he lay on a barbed pillow of brambles and gasped like a landed fish, while at the other side of the fence the police hurtled down the footpath yelling after their suspect.

Catso scarcely heard their commands. It wasn't the police that he was running from: it was the muddied thing that had lifted him up to meet its slitted and chancred face. Now, as he reached the Archway Road, he felt tremors beginning in his limbs. If his legs gave out he was certain it would come for him again, and lay its mouth on his as it already had. Only this time he would not have the strength to scream; the life would be sucked from his lungs. His only hope lay in putting the road between him and his tormentor. The beast's breath loud in his ears, he scaled the crash-barrier, leapt down on to the road, and began across the south-bound carriageway at a run. Halfway across he realized his error. The horror in his head had blinded him to all other risks. A blue Volvo – its driver's mouth a perfect O – bore down on him. He was caught in its headlights like an animal, entranced: two instants later he was struck a glancing blow which threw him across the divide and into the path of an articulated lorry. The second driver had no chance to swerve: the impact split Catso open and tossed him beneath the wheels.

Up in the garden, Karney heard the panic of the brakes, and the policeman, at the bottom of the pathway say: 'Jesus Christ Almighty'. He waited a few seconds, then peered out from his hiding place. The footpath was now deserted, top and bottom. The trees were quite still. From the road below rose the sound of a siren, and that of the officers shouting for oncoming cars to halt. Closer by, somebody was sobbing. He listened intently for a few moments, trying to work out the source of the sobs, before realizing that they were his own. Tears or no, the clamour from below demanded his attention. Something terrible had happened, and he had to see what. But he was afraid to run the gauntlet of the trees, knowing what lay in wait there, so he stood, staring up into the branches, trying to locate the beast. There was neither sound nor movement, however: the trees were dead still. Stifling his fears, he climbed from his hiding place and began to walk down the pathway, his eyes glued to the foliage for the slightest sign of the beast's presence. He could hear the buzz of a gathering crowd. The thought of a press of people comforted him; from now on he would need a place to hide, wouldn't he? Men who'd seen miracles did.

He had reached the spot where Catso had been dragged up into the trees: a litter of leaves and stolen property marked it. Karney's feet wanted to be swift, to pick him up and whisk him away from the place, but some perverse instinct slowed his pace. Was it that he wanted to tempt the knot's child into showing its face? Better, perhaps, to confront it now – in all its foulness – than to live in fear from this moment on, embroidering its countenance and its capacities. But the beast kept itself hidden. If indeed it was still up there in the tree, it twitched not a nail.

Something moved beneath his foot. Karney looked down, and there, almost lost amongst the leaves, was the cord. Catso had been deemed unworthy to carry it apparently. Now – with some clue to its power revealed – it made no effort to pass for natural. It squirmed on the gravel like a serpent in heat, rearing its knotted head to attract Karney's attention. He wanted to ignore its cavorting, but he couldn't. He knew that if *he* didn't pick up the knots, somebody else would, given time:

65

a victim, like himself, of an urge to solve enigmas. Where could such innocence lead, except to another escape perhaps more terrible than the first? No; it was best that he took the knots. At least he was alive to their potential, and so, in part, armoured against it. He bent down, and as he did so the string fairly leapt into his hands, wrapping itself around his fingers so tightly he almost cried out.

'Bastard,' he said.

The string coiled itself around his hand, weaving its length between his fingers in an ecstasy of welcome. He raised his hand to watch its performance better. His concern for the events on the Archway Road had suddenly, almost miraculously, evaporated. What did such petty concerns matter? It was only life and death. Better to make his getaway now, while he could.

Above his head, a branch shook. He unglued his eyes from the knots and squinted up into the tree. With the cord restored to him his trepidation, like his fears, had evaporated.

'Show yourself,' he said, 'I'm not like Catso; I'm not afraid. I want to know what you are.'

From its camouflage of leaves the waiting beast leaned down towards Karney and exhaled a single, chilly breath. It smelt of the river at low tide, of vegetation gone to rot. Karney was about to ask it what it was again when he realised that the exhalation *was* the beast's reply. All it could speak of its condition was contained in that bitter and rancid breath. As replies went, it was not lacking in eloquence. Distressed by the images it awoke, Karney backed away from the spot. Wounded, sluggish forms moved behind his eyes, engulfed in a sludge of filth.

A few feet from the tree the spell of the breath broke, and Karney drank the polluted air from the road as though it were clean as the world's morning. He turned his back on the agonies he had sensed, thrust his string-woven hand into his pocket, and began up the pathway. Behind him, the trees were quite still again.

Several dozen spectators had gathered on the bridge to watch proceedings below. Their presence had in turn piqued the curiosity of drivers making their way along Hornsey Lane, some of whom had parked their vehicles and got out to join the throng. The scene beneath the bridge seemed too remote to wake any feelings in Karney. He stood amongst the chattering crowd and gazed down quite dispassionately. He recognized Catso's corpse from his clothes: little else remained of his sometime companion.

In a while, he knew, he would have to mourn. But at present he could feel nothing. After all, Catso was dead, wasn't he? His pain and his confusion at an end. Karney sensed he would be wiser to save his tears for those whose agonies were only just beginning.

And again, the knots.

At home that night, he tried to put them away, but, after the events of the evening they had taken on a fresh glamour. *The knots bound beasts.* How, and why, he couldn't know; nor, curiously, did he much care at the moment. All his life he had accepted that the world was rich with mysteries a mind of his limited grasp had no hope of understanding. That was the only genuine lesson his schooldays had taught: that he was ignorant. This new imponderable was just another to tag onto a long list.

Only one rationale really occurred to him, and that was that somehow Pope had arranged his stealing of the knots in the full knowledge that the loosed beast would revenge itself on the old man's tormentors and it wasn't to be until Catso's cremation, six days later, that Karney was to get some confirmation of that theory. In the interim he kept his fears to himself, reasoning that the less he said about the night's events the less harm they could do him. Talk lent the fantastic credibility: it gave weight to phenomena which he hoped, if left to themselves, would become too frail to survive.

When, the following day, the police came to the house on a routine questioning of Catso's friends, he claimed he knew nothing of the circumstances surrounding the death. Brendan had done the same, and as there had seemingly been no witnesses to offer contrary testimony, Karney was not questioned again. Instead he was left to his thoughts; and the knots.

Once, he saw Brendan. He had expected recriminations; Brendan's belief was that Catso had been running from the police when he was killed, and it had been Karney's lack of concentration that had failed to alert them to the law's proximity. But Brendan made no accusations. He had taken the burden of guilt on to himself with a willingness that almost smacked of appetite; he spoke only of his own failure, not of Karney's. The apparent arbitrariness of Catso's demise had uncovered an unlooked-for tenderness in Brendan, and Karney ached to tell him the whole incredible story from beginning to end. But this was not the time, he sensed. He let Brendan spill his hurt out, and kept his own mouth shut.

And still the knots.

Sometimes he would wake in the middle of the night and feel the cord moving beneath his pillow. Its presence was comforting, its eagerness was not, waking, as it did, a similar eagerness in him. He wanted to touch the remaining knots and examine the puzzles they offered. But he knew that to do so was tempting capitulation: to his own fascination; to their hunger for release. When such temptation arose, he forced himself to remember the pathway, and the beast in the trees; to awake again the harrowing thoughts that had come with the beast's breath. Then, by degrees, remembered distress would cancel present curiosity, and he would leave the cord where it lay. Out of sight, though seldom out of mind.

Dangerous as he knew the knots to be, he couldn't bring himself to burn them. As long as he possessed that modest length of cord he was unique; to relinquish it would be to return to his hitherto nondescript condition. He was not willing to do that, even though he suspected that his daily and intimate association with the cord was systematically weakening his ability to resist its seduction.

Of the thing in the tree he saw nothing: he even began to wonder if he hadn't imagined the whole confrontation. Indeed, given time, his powers to rationalize the truth into non-existence might have won the day completely. But events subsequent to the cremation of Catso put an end to such a convenient option.

Karney had gone to the service alone – and, despite the presence of Brendan, Red and Anelisa – he had left alone. He had little wish to speak with any of the mourners. Whatever words he might once have had to frame the events were becoming more difficult to re-invent as time passed. He hurried away from the crematorium before anyone could approach him to talk, his head bowed against the dusty wind which had brought periods of cloud and bright sunshine in swift succession throughout the day. As he walked, he dug in his pocket for a pack of cigarettes. The cord, waiting there as ever, welcomed his fingers in its usual ingratiating manner. He disentangled it, and took out the cigarettes, but the wind was too snappy for matches to stay alight, and his hands seemed unable to perform the simple task of masking the flame. He wandered on a little way until he found an alley, and stepped into it to light up. Pope was there, waiting for him.

'Did you send flowers?' the derelict asked.

Karney's instinct was to turn and run. But the sunlit road was no more than yards away; he was in no danger here. And an exchange with the old man might prove informative.

'No flowers?' Pope said.

'No flowers,' Karney returned. 'What are you doing here?'

'Same as you,' Pope replied. 'Came to see the boy burn.' He grinned, the expression, on that wretched, grimy face, was repulsive to a fault. Pope was still the bag of bones that he'd been in the tunnel two weeks previous, but now an air of threat hung about him. Karney was grateful to have the sun at his back.

'And you. To see you,' Pope said.

Karney chose to make no reply. He struck a match and lit his cigarette.

'You've got something that belongs to me,' Pope said. Karney volunteered no guilt. 'I want my knots back, boy, before you do some *real* damage.'

'I don't know what you're talking about,' Karney replied. His gaze concentrated, unwillingly, on Pope's face, drawn into its intricacies. The alleyway, with its piled refuse, twitched. A cloud had apparently drifted over the sun, for Karney's vision, but for the figure of Pope, darkened subtly.

'It was stupid, boy, to try and steal from me. Not that I wasn't easy prey; that was my error, and it won't happen again. I get lonely sometimes, you see. I'm sure you understand. And when I'm lonely I take to drinking.'

Though mere seconds had apparently passed since Karney had lit his cigarette, it had burned down to the filter without his taking a single pull on it. He dropped it, vaguely aware that time, as well as space, was being pulled out of true in the tiny passage.

'It wasn't me,' he muttered: a child's defence in the face of any and every accusation.

'Yes it was,' Pope replied with incontestable authority. 'Let's not waste breath with fabrication. You stole from me, and your colleague has paid the price. You can't undo the harm you've done. But you *can* prevent further harm, if you return to me what's mine. *Now.*'

Karney's hand had strayed to his pocket, without his quite realizing it. He wanted to get out of this trap before it snapped on him; giving Pope what was, after all, rightfully *his* was surely the easiest way to do it. His fingers hesitated, however; why? Because the Methuselah's eyes were so implacable perhaps; because returning the knots into Pope's hands gave him total control over the weapon that had, in effect, killed Catso? But more; even now, with sanity at risk, Karney was loath to give back the only fragment of mystery that had ever come his way. Pope, sensing his disinclination, pressed his cajoling into a higher gear.

'Don't be afraid of me,' he said. 'I won't do you any harm unless you push me to it. I would *much* prefer that we concluded this matter peacefully; more violence, another death even, would only attract attention.'

Is this a killer I'm looking at? Karney thought; so unkempt, so ridiculously feeble. And yet sound contradicted sight; the seed of command Karney had once heard in Pope's voice was now in full flower.

'Do you want money?' Pope asked 'Is that it? Would your pride be best appeased if I offered you something for your troubles?' Karney looked incredulously at Pope's shabbiness. 'Oh,' the old man said, 'I may not look like a moneyed man, but appearances can be deceptive. In fact, that's the rule, not the exception.

71

Take yourself, for instance. You don't look like a dead man, but take it from me, you are as good as dead, boy. I promise you death if you continue to defy me.'

The speech – so measured, so scrupulous – startled Karney, coming as it did from Pope's lips: thereby proving the man's thesis. A fortnight ago they had caught Pope in his cups – confused and vulnerable – but now, sober, the man spoke like a potentate: a lunatic king, perhaps, going amongst the hoi-polloi as a pauper. King? No, *priest* more like. Something in the nature of his authority (in his name, even) suggested a man whose power had never been rooted in mere politics.

'Once more,' he said, 'I request you to give me what's mine.'

He took a step towards Karney. The alleyway was a narrow tunnel, pressing down on their heads. If there was sky above them, Pope had blinded it.

'Give me the knots,' he said. His voice was softly reassuring. The darkness had closed in completely. All Karney could see was the man's mouth: his uneven teeth, his grey tongue. 'Give them to me, thief, or suffer the consequences.'

'Karney?'

Red's voice came from another world. It was just a few paces away – the voice, sunlight, wind – but for a long moment Karney struggled to locate it again.

'Karney?'

He dragged his consciousness out from between Pope's teeth and forced his face round to look at the road. Red was there, standing in the sun, Anelisa at his side. Her blonde hair shone.

'What's going on?'

'Leave us alone,' Pope said. 'We've got business, he and I.'

'You've got business with *him*?' Red asked of Karney.

Before Karney could reply Pope said: 'Tell him. Tell him, Karney, you want to speak to me alone.'

Red threw a glance over Karney's shoulder towards the old man. 'You want to tell me what's going on?' he said.

Karney's tongue was labouring to find a response, but failing. The sunlight was so far away; every time a cloud-shadow passed across the street he feared the light would be extinguished permanently. His lips worked silently to express his fear.

'You all right?' Red asked. '*Karney*? Can you hear me?'

Karney nodded. The darkness that held him was beginning to lift.

'Yes . . .' he said.

Suddenly, Pope threw himself at Karney, his hands scrabbling desperately for his pockets. The impact of the attack carried Karney, still in a stupor, back against the wall of the alleyway. He fell sideways against a pile of crates. They, and he, toppled over, and Pope, his grip on Karney too fierce to be dislodged, fell too. All the preceding calm – the gallows humour, the circumspect threats – had evaporated; he was again the idiot derelict, spouting insanities. Karney felt the man's hands tearing at his clothes and raking his skin in his bid for the knots. The words he was shouting into Karney's face were no longer comprehensible.

Red stepped into the alley and attempted to drag the old man, by coat or hair or beard, whichever handhold presented itself, off his victim. It was easier said than done; the assault had all the fury of a fit. But Red's superior strength won out. Spitting nonsenses, Pope was pulled to his feet. Red held on to him as if he were a mad dog.

'Get up . . .' he told Karney, 'get out of his reach.'

Karney staggered to his feet amongst the tinder of

73

crates. In the scant seconds of his attack Pope had done considerable damage: Karney was bleeding in half a dozen places. His clothes had been savaged; his shirt ripped beyond repair. Tentatively, he put his hand to his raked face; the scratches were raised like ritual scars.

Red pushed Pope against the wall. The derelict was still apoplectic, eyes wild. A stream of invective – a jumble of English and gibberish – was flung in Red's face. Without pausing in his tirade Pope made another attempt to attack Karney, but this time Red's hand-hold prevented the claws from making contact. Red hauled Pope out of the alley and into the road.

'Your lip's bleeding,' Anelisa said, looking at Karney with plain disgust. Karney could taste the blood: salty and hot. He put the back of his hand to his mouth. It came away scarlet.

'Good thing we came after you,' she said.

'Yeah,' he returned, not looking at the woman. He was ashamed of the showing he'd made in the face of the vagrant, and knew she must be laughing at his inability to defend himself. Her family were villains to a man, her father a folk-hero amongst thieves.

Red came back in from the street. Pope had gone.

'What was all that about?' he demanded to know, taking a comb from his jacket pocket and re-establishing his quiff.

'Nothing,' Karney replied.

'Don't give me shit,' Red said. 'He claims you stole something from him. Is that right?'

Karney glanced across at Anelisa. But for her presence he might have been willing to tell Red everything, there and then. She returned his glance and seemed to read his thoughts. Shrugging, she moved out of ear-shot, kicking through the demolished crates as she went.

'He's got it in for us all, Red,' Karney said.

'What are you talking about?'

74

Karney looked down at his bloody hand. Even with Anelisa out of the way, the words to explain what he suspected were slow in coming.

'Catso . . .' he began.

'What about him?'

'He was running, Red.'

Behind him, Anelisa expelled an irritated sigh. This was taking longer than she'd temper for.

'Red,' she said, 'we'll be late.'

'Wait a minute,' Red told her sharply, and turned his attention back to Karney. 'What do you mean: about Catso?'

'The old man's not what he seems. He's not a vagrant.'

'Oh? What is he?' A note of sarcasm had crept back into Red's voice: for Anelisa's benefit, no doubt. The girl had tired of discretion, and had wandered back to join Red. 'What is he, Karney?'

Karney shook his head. What was the use of trying to explain a *part* of what had happened? Either he attempted the entire story, or nothing at all. Silence was easier.

'It doesn't matter,' he said, flatly.

Red gave him a puzzled look, then, when there was no clarification forthcoming, said: 'If you've got something to tell me about Catso, Karney, I'd like to hear it. You know where I live.'

'Sure,' said Karney.

'I mean it,' Red said, 'about talking.'

'Thanks.'

'Catso was a good mate, you know? Bit of a piss-artist, but we've all had our moments, eh? He shouldn't have died, Karney. It was wrong.'

'Red —'

'She's calling you.' Anelisa had wandered out into the street.

'She's always calling me. I'll see you around, Karney.'

'Yeah.'

Red patted Karney's stinging cheek and followed Anelisa out into the sun. Karney made no move to follow them. Pope's assault had left him trembling; he intended to wait in the alleyway until he'd regained a gloss of composure, at least. Seeking reassurance of the knots, he put his hand into his jacket pocket. It was empty. He checked his other pockets. They too were empty, and yet he was certain that the old man's grasp had failed to get near the cord. Perhaps they had slipped out of hiding during the struggle. Karney began to scour the alley, and when the first search failed, followed with a second and a third; but by that time he knew the operation was lost. Pope *had* succeeded after all. By stealth or chance, he had regained the knots.

With startling clarity, Karney remembered standing on Suicides' Leap, looking down on to the Archway Road, Catso's body sprawled below at the centre of a network of lights and vehicles. He had felt so *removed* from the tragedy: viewing it with all the involvement of a passing bird. Now – suddenly – he was shot from the sky. He was on the ground, and wounded, waiting hopelessly for the terrors to come. He tasted blood from his split lip and wondered, wishing the thought would vanish even as it formed, if Catso had died immediately, or if he too had tasted blood as he'd lain there on the tarmac, looking up at the people on the bridge who had yet to learn how close death was.

He returned home via the most populated route he could plan. Though this exposed his disreputable state to the stares of matrons and policemen alike he preferred their disapproval to chancing the empty streets away from the major thoroughfares. Once home, he bathed his scratches and put on a fresh set of clothes, then sat in front of the television for a while to allow his limbs to stop shaking. It was late afternoon, and the programmes were all children's fare: a tone of queasy optimism infected every channel. He watched the banalities with his eyes but not with his mind, using the respite to try and find the words to describe all that had happened to him. The imperative was now to warn Red and Brendan. With Pope in control of the knots it could only be a matter of time before some beast – worse, perhaps, than the thing in the trees – came looking for them all. Then it would be too late for explanations. He knew the other two would be contemptuous, but he would sweat to convince them, however ridiculous he ended up looking in the process. Perhaps his tears and his panic would move them the way his impoverished vocabulary never could. About five after five, before his mother returned home from work, he slipped out of the house and went to find Brendan.

Anelisa took the piece of string she'd found in the alleyway out of her pocket and examined it. Why she had bothered to pick it up at all she wasn't certain, but somehow it had found its way into her hand. She played with one of the knots, risking her long nails in doing so. She had half a dozen better things to be doing with her early evening. Red had gone to buy drink and cigarettes and she had promised herself a leisurely, scented bath before he returned. But the knot wouldn't take that long to untie, she was certain of that. Indeed, it seemed almost eager to be undone: she had the strangest sensation of movement in it. And more intriguing yet, there were colours in the knot – she could see glints of crimson and violet. Within a few minutes, she had forgotten the bath entirely; it could wait. Instead she concentrated on the conundrum at her fingertips. After only a few minutes she began to see the light.

Karney told Brendan the story as best he could. Once he had taken the plunge and begun it from the beginning, he discovered it had its own momentum, which carried him through to the present tense with relatively little hesitation. He finished, saying:

'I know it sounds wild, but it's all true.'

Brendan didn't believe a word; that much was apparent in his blank stare. But there was more than disbelief on the scarred face. Karney couldn't work out what it was until Brendan took hold of his shirt. Only then did he see the depth of Brendan's fury.

'You don't think it's bad enough that Catso's dead,' he seethed, 'you have to come here telling me this shit.'

'It's the truth.'

'And where are these fucking knots now?'

'I told you: the old man's got them. He took them this afternoon. He's going to kill us, Bren. I know it.'

Brendan let Karney go. 'Tell you what I'm going to do,' he said magnanimously, 'I'm going to forget you told me any of this.'

'You don't understand –'

'I *said*: I'm going to forget you uttered one word. All right? Now you just get the fuck out of here and take your funny stories with you.'

Karney didn't move.

'*You hear me?*' Brendan shouted. Karney caught sight of a telltale fullness at the edge of Brendan's eyes. The anger was camouflage – barely adequate – for a grief he had no mechanism to prevent. In Brendan's present mood neither fear nor argument would convince him of the truth. Karney stood up.

'I'm sorry,' he said, 'I'll go.'

Brendan shook his head, face down. He did not raise it again, but left Karney to make his own way out. There was only Red now; he was the final court of appeal.

The story, now told, could be told again, couldn't it? Repetition would be easy. Already turning the words over in his head, he left Brendan to his tears.

Anelisa heard Red come in through the front door; heard him call out a word; heard him call it again. The word was familiar, but it took her several seconds of fevered thought to recognize it as her own name.

'Anelisa!' he called again. 'Where are you?'

Nowhere, she thought. I'm the invisible woman. Don't come looking for me; please God, just leave me alone. She put her hand to her mouth, to stop her teeth from chattering. She had to stay absolutely still, absolutely silent. If she stirred so much as a hair's breadth it would hear her and come for her. The only safety lay in tying herself into a tiny ball and sealing her mouth with her palm.

Red began to climb the stairs. Doubtless Anelisa was in the bath, singing to herself. The woman loved water as she loved little else. It was not uncommon for her to spend hours immersed, her breasts breaking surface like two dream islands. Four steps from the landing, he heard a noise in the hallway below: a cough, or something like it. Was she playing some game with him? He about turned and descended, moving more stealthily now. Almost at the bottom of the stairs his gaze fell on a piece of cord which had been dropped on one of the steps. He picked it up and briefly puzzled over the single knot in its length, before the noise came again. This time he did not pretend to himself that it was Anelisa. He held his breath, waiting for another prompt from along the hallway. When none came he dug into the side of his boot and pulled out his flick-knife, a weapon he had carried about his person since the tender age of eleven. An adolescent's weapon, Anelisa's father had advised him; but now, advancing along the hallway to

the living room, he thanked the patron saint of blades
he had not taken the old felon's advice.

The room was gloomy. Evening was on the house,
shuttering up the windows. Red stood for a long while
in the doorway, anxiously watching the interior for
movement. Then the noise again; not a single sound
this time, but a whole series of them. The source, he
now realised to his relief, was not human. It was a dog
most likely, wounded in a fight. Nor was the sound
coming from the room in front of him, but from the
kitchen beyond. His courage bolstered by the fact that
the intruder was merely an animal, he reached for the
light switch and flipped it on.

The helter-skelter of events he initiated in so doing
occurred in a breathless sequence that occupied no
more than a dozen seconds, yet he lived each one
in the minutest detail. In the first second, as the
light came on, he saw something move across the
kitchen floor; in the next, he was walking towards
it, knife still in hand. The third brought the animal
– alerted to his planned aggression – out of hiding. It
ran to meet him, a blur of glistening flesh. Its sudden
proximity was overpowering: its size, the heat off its
steaming body, its vast mouth expelling a breath like
rot. Red took the fourth and fifth seconds to avoid its
first lunge, but on the sixth it found him. Its raw arms
snatched at his body. He slashed out with his knife, and
opened a wound in it, but it closed in and took him in a
lethal embrace. More through accident than intention,
the flick-knife plunged into its flesh, and liquid heat
splashed up into Red's face: he scarcely noticed. His
last three seconds were upon him: the weapon, slick
with blood, slid from his grasp and was left embedded
in the beast. Unarmed, he attempted to squirm from
its clasp, but before he could slide out of harm's way
the great unfinished head was pressing towards him –

the maw a tunnel – and sucked one solid breath from his lungs. It was the only breath Red possessed. His brain, deprived of oxygen, threw a firework display in celebration of his imminent departure: roman candles, star shells, catherine wheels. The pyrotechnics were all too brief; too soon, the darkness.

Upstairs, Anelisa listened to the chaos of sound and tried to piece it together, but she could not. Whatever had happened, however, it had ended in silence. Red did not come looking for her. But then nor did the beast. Perhaps, she thought, they had killed each other. The simplicity of this solution pleased her. She waited in her room until hunger and boredom got the better of trepidation, and then went downstairs. Red was lying where the cord's second off-spring had dropped him, his eyes wide open to watch the fireworks. The beast itself squatted in the far corner of the room, a ruin of a thing. Seeing it, she backed away from Red's body towards the door. It made no attempt to move towards her, but simply followed her with deep-set eyes, its breathing coarse, its few movements sluggish.

She would go to find her father, she decided, and fled the house, leaving the front door ajar.

It was still ajar half an hour later, when Karney arrived. Though he had fully intended to go straight to Red's home after leaving Brendan, his courage had faltered. Instead, he had wandered – without conscious planning – to the bridge over the Archway Road. He had stood there for a long space watching the traffic below and drinking from the half bottle of vodka he had bought on the Holloway Road. The purchase had cleared him of cash, but the spirits, on his empty stomach, had been potent, and clarified his thinking. They would all die, he had concluded. Maybe the fault was his, for stealing the cord in the first place; more probably Pope would have punished them anyway for their crimes against his person. The best they might now hope – *he* might hope – was a smidgen of comprehension. That would almost be enough, his spirit-slurred brain decided: just to die a little less ignorant of mysteries than he'd been born. Red would understand.

Now he stood on the step and called the man's name. There came no answering shout. The vodka in his system made him impudent and, calling for Red again, he stepped into the house. The hallway was in darkness, but a light burned in one of the far rooms and he made his way towards it. The atmosphere in the house was sultry, like the interior of a palm-house. It became warmer still in the living room, where Red was losing body-heat to the air.

Karney stared down at him long enough to register that he was holding the cord in his left hand, and that only one knot remained in it. Perhaps Pope had been here, and for some reason left the knots behind. However it had come about, their presence in Red's hand offered a chance for life. This time, he swore as he approached the body, he would destroy the cord once and for all. Burn it and scatter the ashes to the four winds. He stooped to remove it from Red's grip. It sensed his nearness and slipped, blood-sleek, out of the dead man's hand and up into Karney's, where it wove itself between his digits, leaving a trail behind it. Sickened, Karney stared at the final knot. The process which had taken him so much painstaking effort to initiate now had its own momentum. With the second knot untied the third was virtually loosening itself. It still required a human agent apparently – why else did it leap so readily into his hand? – but it was already close to solving its own riddle. It was imperative he destroyed it quickly, before it succeeded.

Only then did he become aware that he was not alone. Besides the dead, there was a living presence close by.

He looked up from the cavorting knot as somebody spoke to him. The words made no sense. They were scarcely words at all, more a sequence of wounded sounds. Karney remembered the breath of the thing on the footpath, and the ambiguity of the feelings it had engendered in him. Now the same ambiguity moved him again: with the rising fear came a sense that the voice of the beast spoke *loss*, whatever its language. A rumour of pity moved in him.

'Show yourself,' he said, not knowing whether it would understand or not.

A few tremulous heartbeats passed, and then it emerged from the far door. The light in the living room was good, and Karney's eyesight sharp, but the beast's anatomy defied his comprehension. There was something simian in its flayed, palpitating form, but sketchy, as if it had been born prematurely. Its mouth opened to speak another sound; its eyes, buried beneath the bleeding slab of a brow, were unreadable. It began to shamble out of its hiding place across the room towards him, each drooping step it took tempting his cowardice. When it reached Red's corpse, it stopped, raised one of its ragged limbs, and indicated a place in the crook of its neck. Karney saw the knife: Red's he guessed. Was it attempting to justify the killing, he wondered?

'What are you?' he asked it. The same question.

It shook its heavy head back and forth. A long, low moan issued from its mouth. Then, suddenly, it raised its arm and pointed directly at Karney. In so doing it let light fall fully on its face, and Karney could make out the eyes beneath the louring brow: twin gems trapped in the wounded ball of its skull. Their brilliance, and their lucidity, turned Karney's stomach over. And still it pointed at him.

'What do you want?' he asked it. 'Tell me what you want.'

It dropped its peeled limb and made to step across the body towards Karney, but it had no chance to make its intentions clear. A shout from the front door froze it in its lolling tracks.

'Anybody in?' the inquirer wanted to know.

Its face registered panic – the too-human eyes rolled in their raw sockets – and it turned away, retreating towards the kitchen. The visitor, whoever he was, called again: his voice was closer. Karney stared down at the corpse, and at his bloody hand, juggling his options, then started across the room and through the door into the kitchen. The beast had already gone: the back door stood wide open. Behind him, Karney heard the visitor utter some half-formed prayer at seeing Red's remains. He hesitated in the shadows: was this covert escape wise? Did it not do more to incriminate him than staying and trying to find a way to the truth? The knot, still moving in his hand, finally decided him: its destruction had to be his priority. In the living room, the visitor was dialling the emergency services; using his panicked monologue as cover, Karney crept the remaining yards to the back door and fled.

'Somebody's been on the phone for you,' his mother called down from the top of the stairs, 'he's woken me twice already. I told him I didn't –'

'I'm sorry, Mam. Who was it?'

'Wouldn't say. I told him not to ring back. You tell him, if he calls again, I don't want people ringing up at this time of night. Some people have to get up for work in the morning.'

'Yes, Mam.'

His mother disappeared from the landing, and returned to her solitary bed; the door closed. Karney stood, trembling, in the hallway below, his hand clenched around the knot in his pocket. It was still moving, turning itself over and over against the confines of his palm, seeking some space, however small, in which to loosen itself. But he was giving it no latitude. He rummaged for the vodka he'd bought earlier in the evening, manipulated the top off the bottle single-handed, and drank. As he took a second, galling mouthful, the telephone rang. He put down the bottle and picked up the receiver.

'Hello?'

The caller was in a phone box; the pips sounded, money was deposited, and a voice said: 'Karney?'

'Yes?'

'For Christ's sake, he's going to kill me.'

'Who is this?'

'Brendan.' The voice was not like Brendan's at all; too shrill, too fearful. 'He'll kill me if you don't come.'

'Pope? Is it Pope?'

'He's out of his mind. You've got to come to the breaker's yard, at the top of the hill. Give him –'

The line went dead. Karney put the receiver down. In his hand the cord was performing acrobatics. He opened his hand; in the dim light from the landing the remaining knot shimmered. At its heart, as at the hearts of the other two knots, glints of colour promised themselves. He closed his fist again, picked up the vodka bottle, and went back out.

The breaker's yard had once boasted a large and perpetually irate Doberman pinscher, but the dog had developed a tumour the previous spring and savaged its owner. It had subsequently been destroyed, and no replacement bought. The corrugated iron wall was consequently easy to breach. Karney clambered over and down on to the cinder and gravel strewn ground on the other side. A floodlight at the front gate threw illumination on to the collection of vehicles, both domestic and commercial, which was assembled in the yard. Most were beyond salvation: rusted lorries and tankers, a bus which had apparently hit a low bridge at speed, a rogue's gallery of cars, lined up or piled upon each other, every one an accident casualty. Beginning at the gate, Karney began a systematic search of the yard, trying as best he could to keep his footsteps light, but he could find no sign of Pope or his prisoner at the north-west end of the yard. Knot in hand, he began to advance down the enclosure, the reassuring light at the gate dwindling with every step he took. A few paces on, he caught sight of flames between two of the vehicles. He stood still, and tried to interpret the intricate play of shadow and firelight. Behind him, he heard movement, and turned, anticipating with every heartbeat a cry, a blow. None came. He scoured the yard at his back – the image of the yellow flame dancing on his retina – but whatever had moved was now still again.

'Brendan?' he whispered, looking back towards the fire.

In a slab of shadow in front of him a figure moved, and Brendan stumbled out and fell to his knees in the cinders a few feet from where Karney stood. Even in the deceptive light Karney could see that Brendan was the worse for punishment. His shirt was smeared with stains too dark to be anything but blood; his face was contorted with present pain, or the anticipation of it. When Karney walked towards him he shied away like a beaten animal.

'It's me. It's Karney.'

Brendan raised his bruised head. 'Make him stop.'

'It'll be all right.'

'Make him stop. Please.'

Brendan's hands went up to his neck. A collar of rope encircled his throat; a leash led off from it into the darkness between two vehicles. There, holding the other end of the leash, stood Pope. His eyes glimmered in the shadows, although they had no source to glean their light from.

'You were wise to come,' Pope said. 'I would have killed him.'

'Let him go,' Karney said.

Pope shook his head. 'First the knot.' He stepped out of hiding. Somehow Karney had expected him to have sloughed off his guise as a derelict and show his true face – whatever that might be – but he had not. He was dressed in the same shabby garb as he had always worn; but his control of the situation was incontestable. He gave a short tug on the rope, and Brendan collapsed, choking, to the ground, hands tugging vainly at the noose closing about his throat.

'Stop it,' Karney said, 'I've got the knot, damn you. Don't kill him.'

'Bring it to me.'

Even as Karney took a step towards the old man something cried out in the labyrinth of the yard. Karney recognized the sound; so did Pope. It was unmistakably the voice of the flayed beast that had killed Red, and it was close by. Pope's besmirched face blazed with fresh urgency.

'Quickly!' he said, 'or I kill him.' He had drawn a gutting knife from his coat. Pulling on the leash, he coaxed Brendan close.

The complaint of the beast rose in pitch.

'*The knot!*' Pope said. '*To me!*' He stepped towards Brendan, and put the blade to the prisoner's close-cropped head.

'Don't,' said Karney, 'just take the knot.' But before he could draw another breath something moved at the corner of his eye, and his wrist was snatched in a scalding grip. Pope let out a shout of anger, and Karney turned to see the scarlet beast at his side, meeting his gaze with a haunted stare. Karney wrestled to loose its hold, but it shook its ravaged head.

'Kill it!' Pope yelled. *'Kill it!'*

The beast glanced across at Pope, and for the first time Karney saw an unequivocal look in its pale eyes: naked loathing. Then Brendan issued a sharp cry, and Karney looked his way in time to see the gutting knife slide into his cheek. Pope withdrew the blade, and let Brendan's corpse pitch forward; before it had struck the ground he was crossing towards Karney, murderous intention in every stride. The beast, fear in its throat, released Karney's arm in time for him to side-step Pope's first thrust. Beast and man divided, and ran. Karney's heels slithered in the loose cinders and for an instant he felt Pope's shadow on him, but slid from the path of the second cut with millimetres to spare.

'You can't get out,' he heard Pope boast as he ran. The old man was so confident of his trap he wasn't even giving chase. 'You're on my territory, boy. There's no way out.'

Karney ducked into hiding between two vehicles and started to weave his way back towards the gate, but somehow he'd lost all sense of orientation. One parade of rusted hulks let onto another, so similar as to be indistinguishable. Wherever the maze led him there seemed to be no way out; he could no longer see the lamp at the gate, or Pope's fire at the far end of the yard. It was all one hunting-ground, and he the prey; and everywhere this daedal path led him, Pope's voice followed close as his heartbeat. 'Give up the knot, boy,' it said, 'give it up and I won't feed you your eyes.'

Karney was terrified; but so, he sensed, was Pope. The cord was not an assassination tool, as Karney had always believed. Whatever its rhyme or reason, the old man did *not* have mastery of it. In that fact lay what slim chance of survival remained. The time had come to untie the final knot: untie it and take the consequences. Could they be any worse than death at Pope's hands?

Karney found an adequate refuge alongside a burnt out lorry, slid down into a squatting position, and opened his fist. Even in the darkness, he could feel the knot working to decipher itself; he aided it as best he could.

Again, Pope spoke: 'Don't do it, boy,' he said, pretending humanity. 'I know what you're thinking and believe me it will be the end of you.'

Karney's hands seemed to have sprouted thumbs, no longer the equal of the problem. His mind was a gallery of death portraits: Catso on the road, Red on the carpet, Brendan slipping from Pope's grip as the knife slid from his head. He forced the images away, marshalling his beleaguered wits as best he could. Pope had curtailed his monologue. Now the only sound in the yard was the distant hum of traffic; it came from a world Karney doubted he would see again. He fumbled at the knot like a man at a locked door with a handful of keys, trying one and then the next and then the next, all the while knowing that the night is pressing on his back. *'Quickly, quickly,'* he urged himself. But his former dexterity had utterly deserted him.

And then a hiss as the air was sliced, and Pope had found him – his face triumphant as he delivered the killing strike. Karney rolled from his squatting position, but the blade caught his upper arm, opening a wound that ran from shoulder to elbow. The pain made him quick, and the second strike struck the cab of the lorry, winning sparks not blood. Before Pope could stab again Karney was dodging away, blood pulsing from his arm. The old man gave chase, but Karney was fleeter. He ducked behind one of the coaches, and, as Pope panted after him, slipped into hiding beneath the vehicle. Pope ran past as Karney bit back a sob of pain. The wound

he had sustained effectively incapacitated his left hand.
Drawing his arm into his body to minimize the stress on
his slashed muscle, he tried to finish the wretched work
he had begun on the knot, using his teeth in place of
a second hand. Splashes of white light were appearing
in front of him: unconsciousness was not far distant.
He breathed deeply and regularly through his nostrils
as his fevered fingers pulled at the knot. He could no
longer see, nor could scarcely feel, the cord in his hand.
He was working blind, as he had on the footpath, and
now, as then, his instincts began to work for him. The
knot started to dance at his lips, eager for release. It was
mere moments from solution.

In his devotion, he failed to see the arm reach for him
until he was being hauled out of his sanctuary and was
staring up into Pope's shining eyes.

'No more games,' the old man said, and loosed his
hold on Karney to snatch the cord from between his
teeth. Karney attempted to move a few tortuous inches
to avoid Pope's grasp, but the pain in his arm crippled
him. He fell back, letting out a cry on impact.

'Out go your eyes,' said Pope and the knife descended.
The blinding blow never landed, however. A wounded
form emerged from hiding behind the old man and
snatched at the tails of his gabardine. Pope regained his
balance in moments and spun around. The knife found
his antagonist, and Karney opened his pain-blurred eyes
to see the flayed beast reeling backwards, its cheek
slashed open to the bone. Pope followed through to
finish the slaughter, but Karney didn't wait to watch.
He reached up for purchase on the wreck, and hauled
himself to his feet, the knot still clenched between his
teeth. Behind him, Pope cursed, and Karney knew he
had forsaken the kill to follow. Knowing the pursuit was
already lost, he staggered out from between the vehicles
into the open yard. In which direction was the gate? He

had no idea. His legs belonged to a comedian, not to him; they were rubber jointed, useless for everything but pratfalls. Two steps forward and his knees gave out. The smell of petrol-soaked cinders came up to meet him.

Despairing, he put his good hand up to his mouth. His fingers found a loop of cord. He pulled, *hard*, and miraculously the final hitch of the knot came free. He spat the cord from his mouth as a surging heat roasted his lips; it fell to the ground, its final seal broken, and from its core the last of its prisoners materialized. It appeared on the cinders like a sickly infant, its limbs vestigial, its bald head vastly too big for its withered body, the flesh of which was pale to the point of translucence. It flapped its palsied arms in a vain attempt to right itself as Pope stepped towards it, eager to slit its defenceless throat. Whatever Karney had hoped from the third knot it hadn't been this scrag of life; it revolted him.

And then it spoke. Its voice was no mewling infant's but that of a grown man, albeit spoken from a babe's mouth.

'To me!' it called. '*Quickly.*'

As Pope reached down to murder the child the air of the yard filled with the stench of mud, and the shadows disgorged a spiny, low-bellied thing, which slid across the ground towards him. Pope stepped back as the creature – as unfinished in its reptilian way as its simian brother – closed on the strange infant. Karney fully expected it to devour the morsel, but the pallid child raised its arms in welcome as the beast from the first knot curled about it. As it did so the second beast showed its ghastly face, moaning its pleasure. It laid its hands on the child and drew the wasted body up into its capacious arms, completing an unholy family of reptile, ape and child.

The union was not over yet, however. Even as the

91

three creatures assembled their bodies began to fray, unravelling into ribbons of pastel matter; and even as their anatomies began to dissolve the strands were beginning a fresh configuration, filament entwining with filament. They were tying another knot, random and yet inevitable; more elaborate by far than any Karney had set fingers on. A new and perhaps insoluble puzzle was appearing from the pieces of the old, but – where *they* had been inchoate – this one would be finished and whole. What though; *what*?

As the skein of nerves and muscle moved towards its final condition, Pope took his moment. He rushed forward, his face wild in the lustre of the union, and thrust his gutting knife into the heart of the knot. But the attack was mistimed. A limb of ribboned light uncurled from the body and wrapped itself around Pope's wrist. The gabardine ignited; Pope's flesh began to burn. He screeched, and dropped the weapon. The limb released him, returning itself into the weave and leaving the old man to stagger backwards, nursing his smoking arm. He looked to be losing his wits; he shook his head to and fro pitifully. Momentarily, his eyes found Karney, and a glimmer of guile crept back into them. He reached for the boy's injured arm, and hugged him close. Karney cried out, but Pope, careless of his captive, dragged Karney away from where the wreathing was nearing its end and into the safety of the labyrinth.

'He won't harm me,' Pope was saying to himself, 'not with you. Always had a weakness for children.' He pushed Karney ahead of him. 'Just get the papers . . . then away.'

Karney scarcely knew if he was alive or dead: he had no strength left to fight Pope off. He just went with the old man, half crawling much of the time, until they reached Pope's destination: a car which was buried behind a heap of rusted vehicles. It had no wheels;

a bush which had grown through the chassis occupied the driver's seat. Pope opened the back door, muttering his satisfaction, and bent into the interior, leaving Karney slumped against the wing. Unconsciousness was a teasing moment away; Karney longed for it. But Pope had use for him yet. Retrieving a small book from its niche beneath the passenger seat Pope whispered: 'Now we must go. We've got business.' Karney groaned as he was pressed forward.

'Close your mouth,' Pope said, embracing him, 'my brother has ears.'

'Brother?' Karney murmured, trying to make sense of what Pope had let slip.

'Spellbound,' Pope said, 'until you.'

'Beasts,' Karney muttered, the mingled images of reptiles and apes assailing him.

'Human,' Pope replied. 'Evolution's the knot, boy.'

'*Human*,' Karney said and as the syllables left him his aching eyes caught sight of a gleaming form on the car at his tormentor's back. Yes; it *was* human. Still wet from its re-birth, its body running with inherited wounds, but triumphantly human. Pope saw the recognition in Karney's eyes. He seized hold of him and was about to use the limp body as shield when his brother intervened. The rediscovered man reached down from the height of the roof and caught hold of Pope by his narrow neck. The old man shrieked, and tore himself loose, darting away across the cinders, but the other gave howling chase, pursuing him out of Karney's range.

From a long way off, Karney heard Pope's last plea as his brother overtook him, and then the words curved up into a scream Karney hoped never to hear the equal of again. After that, silence. The sibling did not return; for which, curiosity notwithstanding, Karney was grateful.

When, several minutes later, he mustered sufficient energy to make his way out of the yard – the light burned at the gate again, a beacon to the perplexed – he found Pope lying, face down, on the gravel. Even if he had possessed the strength, which he did not, a small fortune could not have persuaded Karney to turn the body over. Enough to see how the dead man's hands had dug into the ground in his torment, and how the bright coils of innards, once so neatly looped in his abdomen, spilled out from beneath him. The book Pope had been at such pains to retrieve lay at his side. Karney stooped, head spinning, to pick it up. It was, he felt, small recompense for the night of terrors he had endured. The near future would bring questions he could never hope to answer, accusations he had pitifully little defence against. But, by the light of the gateside lamp, he found the stained pages more rewarding than he'd anticipated. Here, copied out in a meticulous hand, and accompanied by elaborate diagrams, were the theorems of Pope's forgotten science: the designs of knots for the securing of love, and the winning of status; hitches to divide souls and bind them; for the making of fortunes and children; for the world's ruin.

After a brief perusal, he scaled the gate and clambered over onto the street. It was, at such an hour, deserted. A few lights burned in the council estate opposite; rooms where the sick waited out the hours until morning. Rather than ask any more of his exhausted limbs Karney decided to wait where he was until he could flag down a vehicle to take him where he might tell his story. He had plenty to occupy him. Although his body was numb and his head woozy, he felt more lucid than he ever had. He came to the mysteries on the pages of Pope's forbidden book as to an oasis. Drinking deeply, he looked forward with rare exhilaration to the pilgrimage ahead.

REVELATIONS

T HERE HAD BEEN talk of tornadoes in Amarillo; of
cattle, cars, and sometimes entire houses lifted up
and dashed to the earth again, of whole communities
laid waste in a few devastating moments. Perhaps that
was what made Virginia so uneasy tonight. Either that,
or the accumulated fatigue of travelling so many empty
highways with just the deadpan skies of Texas for scen-
ery, and nothing to look forward to at the end of the
next leg of the journey but another round of hymns
and hellfire. She sat, her spine aching, in the back
of the black Pontiac, and tried her best to get some
sleep. But the hot, still air clung about her thin neck
and gave her dreams of suffocation; so she gave up her
attempts to rest and contented herself with watching the
wheat-fields pass and counting the grain elevators bright
against the thunderheads that were beginning to gather in
the north-east.

In the front of the vehicle Earl sang to himself as he
drove. Beside her, John – no more than two feet away

from her but to all intents and purposes a million miles' distant – studied the Epistles of St Paul, and murmured the words as he read. Then, as they drove through Pantex Village ('They build the warheads here,' Earl had said cryptically, then said no more) the rain began. It came down suddenly, as evening was beginning to fall, lending darkness to darkness, almost instantly plunging the Amarillo-Pampa Highway into watery night.

Virginia wound up her window; the rain, though refreshing, was soaking her plain blue dress, the only one John approved of her wearing at meetings. Now there was nothing to look at beyond the glass. She sat, the unease growing in her with every mile they covered to Pampa, listening to the vehemence of the downpour on the roof of the car, and to her husband speaking in whispers at her side:

'*Wherefore he saith, Awake thou that sleepest, and rise from the dead, and Christ shall give thee light.*

'*See then that ye walk circumspectly, not as fools, but as wise,*

'*Redeeming the time, because the days are evil.*'

He sat, as ever, upright, the same dog-eared, soft-backed Bible he'd been using for years open in his lap. He surely knew the passages he was reading by heart; he quoted them often enough, and with such a mixture of familiarity and freshness that the words might have been his, not Paul's, new-minted from his own mouth. That passion and vigour would in time make John Gyer America's greatest evangelist, Virginia had no doubt of that. During the gruelling, hectic weeks of the Tri-State Tour her husband had displayed unprecedented confidence and maturity. His message had lost none of its vehemence with this newfound professionalism – it was still that old-fashioned mixture of damnation and redemption that he always propounded – but now he had complete control of his gifts, and in town after town

– in Oklahoma and New Mexico and now in Texas – the faithful had gathered to listen in their hundreds and thousands, eager to come again into God's Kingdom. In Pampa, thirty-five miles from here, they would already be assembling, despite the rain, determined to have a grandstand view when the crusader arrived. They would have brought their children, their savings, and, most of all, their hunger for forgiveness.

But forgiveness was for tomorrow. First they had to *get* to Pampa, and the rain was worsening. Earl had given up his singing once the storm began, and was concentrating all his attentions on the road ahead. Sometimes he would sigh to himself, and stretch in his seat. Virginia tried not to concern herself with the way he was driving, but as the torrent became a deluge her anxiety got the better of her. She leaned forward from the back seat and started to peer through the windshield, watching for vehicles coming in the opposite direction. Accidents were common in conditions like these: bad weather, and a tired driver eager to be twenty miles further down the road than he was. At her side John sensed her concern.

'The Lord is with us,' he said, not looking up from the tightly printed pages, though it was by now far too dark for him to read.

'It's a bad night, John,' she said. 'Maybe we shouldn't try to go all the way to Pampa. Earl must be tired.'

'I'm fine,' Earl put in, 'it's not that far.'

'You're tired,' Virginia repeated. 'We all are.'

'Well, we could find a motel, I guess,' Gyer suggested. 'What do you think, Earl?'

Earl shrugged his sizeable shoulders. 'Whatever you say, boss,' he replied, not putting up much of a fight.

Gyer turned to his wife and gently patted the back of her hand. 'We'll find a motel,' he said. 'Earl can call ahead to Pampa and tell them that we'll be with them in the morning. How's that?'

She smiled at him, but he wasn't looking at her.

'I think White Deer's next off the highway,' Earl told Virginia. 'Maybe they'll have a motel.'

In fact, the Cottonwood Motel lay a half mile west of White Deer, in an area of wasteground on the south of US 60, a small establishment with a dead or dying cottonwood tree in the lot between its two low buildings. There were a number of cars already in the motel grounds, and lights burning in most of the rooms; fellow fugitives from the storm presumably. Earl drove into the lot and parked as close to the manager's office as possible, then made a dash across the rain-lashed ground to find out if the place had any rooms for the night. With the engine stilled, the sound of the rain on the roof of the Pontiac was more oppressive than ever.

'I hope there's space for us,' Virginia said, watching the water on the window smear the neon sign. Gyer didn't reply. The rain thundered on overhead. 'Talk to me, John,' she said to him.

'What for?'

She shook her head. 'Never mind.' Strands of hair clung to her slightly clammy forehead; though the rain had come, the heat in the air had not lifted. 'I hate the rain,' she said.

'It won't last all night,' Gyer replied, running a hand through his thick grey hair. It was a gesture he used on the platform as punctuation: pausing between one momentous statement and the next. She knew his rhetoric, both physical and verbal, so well. Sometimes she thought she knew everything about him there was to know; that he had nothing left to tell her that she truly wanted to hear. But then the sentiment was probably mutual: they had long ago ceased to have a marriage

98

recognizable as such. Tonight, as every night on this tour, they would lie in separate beds, and he would sleep that deep, easy sleep that came so readily to him, while she surreptitiously swallowed a pill or two to bring some welcome serenity.

'Sleep,' he had often said, 'is a time to commune with the Lord.' He believed in the efficacy of dreams, though he didn't talk of what he saw in them. The time would come when he would unveil the majesty of his visions, she had no doubt of that; but in the meanwhile he slept alone and kept his counsel, leaving her to whatever secret sorrows she might have. It was easy to be bitter, but she fought the temptation. His destiny was manifest, it was demanded of him by the Lord; and if he was fierce with her he was fiercer still with himself, living by a regime that would have destroyed lesser men, and still chastising himself for his pettiest act of weakness.

At last, Earl appeared from the office, and crossed back to the car at a run. He had three keys.

'Rooms Seven and Eight,' he said, breathlessly, the rain dripping off his brow and nose; 'I got the key to the interconnecting door, too.'

'Good,' said Gyer.

'Last two in the place,' he said. 'Shall I drive the car round? The rooms are in the other building.'

The interior of the two rooms was a hymn to banality. They'd stayed in what seemed like a thousand cells like these, identical down to the sickly orange bedcovers and the light-faded print of the Grand Canyon on the pale green walls. John was insensitive to his surroundings, and always had been, but to Virginia's eyes these rooms were an apt model for Purgatory. Soulless limbos in which nothing of moment had ever happened, nor ever would. There was nothing to mark these rooms out as

99

different from all the others, but there was something different in *her* tonight.

It wasn't talk of tornadoes that had brought this strangeness on. She watched Earl to-ing and fro-ing with the bags, and felt oddly removed from herself, as though she was watching events through a veil denser than the warm rain falling outside the door. She was almost sleep-walking. When John quietly told her which bed would be hers for tonight, she lay down, and tried to control her sense of dislocation by relaxing. It was easier said than done. Somebody had a television on in a nearby room, and the late-night movie was word for word clear through the paper-thin walls.

'Are you all right?'

She opened her eyes. Earl, ever solicitous, was looking down at her. He looked as weary as she felt. His face deeply tanned from standing in the sun at the open-air rallies, looked yellowish rather than its usual healthy brown. He was slightly overweight too, though his bulk married well with his wide, stubborn features.

'Yes, I'm fine, thank you,' she said. 'A little thirsty.'

'I'll see if I can get something for you to drink. They'll probably have a Coke machine.'

She nodded, meeting his eyes. There was a sub-text to this exchange which Gyer, who was sitting at the table making notes for tomorrow's speech, could not know. On and off throughout the tour, Earl had supplied Virginia with pills. Nothing exotic; just tranquillizers to soothe her increasingly jangled nerves. But they – like stimulants, make-up and jewellery – were not looked kindly upon by a man of Gyer's principles, and when, by chance, her husband had discovered the drugs, there had been an ugly scene. Earl had taken the brunt of his employer's ire, for which Virginia was deeply grateful. And, though he was under strict instructions never to repeat the crime, he was soon supplying her again. Their guilt was an almost pleasurable secret between them; she read complicity in his eyes even now, as he did in hers.

'No Coca-Cola,' Gyer said.

'Well, I thought we could make an exception –'

'*Exception?*' Gyer said, his voice taking on a characteristic note of self-regard. Rhetoric was in the air, and Earl cursed his idiot tongue. 'The Lord doesn't give us laws to live by so that we can make *exceptions*, Earl. You know better than that.'

At that moment Earl didn't much care what the Lord did or said. His concern was for Virginia. She was strong he knew, despite her Deep South courtesy, and the accompanying façade of frailty; strong enough to bring them all through the minor crises of the tour, when the Lord had failed to step in and help his agents in the field. But nobody's strength was limitless, and he sensed that she was close to collapse. She gave so much to her husband; of her love and admiration, of her energies and enthusiasm. More than once in the past few weeks Earl had thought that perhaps she deserved better than the man in the pulpit.

'Maybe you could get me some iced water?' she said, looking up at him with lines of fatigue beneath her grey-blue eyes. She was not, by contemporary standards, beautiful: her features were too flawlessly aristocratic. Exhaustion lent them new glamour.

'Iced-water, coming right up,' Earl said, forcing a jovial tone that he had little strength to sustain. He went to the door.

'Why don't you call the office and have someone bring it over?' Gyer suggested as Earl made to leave. 'I want to go through next week's itinerary with you.'

'It's no problem,' Earl said, 'really. Besides, I should call Pampa, and tell them we're delayed,' and he was out of the door and onto the walkway before he could be contradicted.

He needed an excuse to have some time to himself; the atmosphere between Virginia and Gyer was deteriorating by the day, and it was not a pleasant spectacle. He stood for a long moment watching the rain sheet down. The cottonwood tree in the middle of the lot hung its balding head in the fury of the deluge; he knew exactly how it felt.

As he stood on the walkway, wondering how he would be able to keep his sanity in the last eight weeks of the tour, two figures walked from the highway, and crossed the lot. He didn't see them, though the path they took to Room Seven led them directly across his line of vision. They walked through the drenching rain from the waste ground behind the manager's office – where, back in 1955, they had parked their red Buick – and though the rain fell in a steady torrent it left them both untouched. The woman, whose hairstyle had been in and out of fashion twice since the fifties, and whose clothes had the same period look, slowed for a moment to stare at the man who was watching the cottonwood tree with such rapt attention. He had kind eyes, despite his frown. In her time she might have loved such a man, she thought; but then her time had long gone, hadn't it? Buck, her husband, turned back to her – 'Are you coming Sadie?' he wanted to know – and she followed him on to the concrete walkway (it had been wooden the last time she was here) and through the open door of Room Seven.

A chill ran down Earl's back. Too much staring at the rain, he thought; that, and too much fruitless longing. He walked to the end of the patio, steeled himself for the dash across the lot to the office, and counting to three, ran.

Sadie Durning glanced over her shoulder to watch Earl go, then looked back at Buck. The years had not tempered the resentment she felt towards her husband, any more than they'd improved his shifty features or

102

his too-easy laugh. She had not much liked him on June 2nd, 1955, and she didn't much like him now, precisely thirty years on. Buck Durning had the soul of a philanderer, as her father had always warned her. That in itself was not so terrible: it was perhaps the masculine condition. But it had led to such grubby behaviour that eventually she had tired of his endless deceptions. He – unknowing to the last – had taken her low spirits as a cue for a second honeymoon. This phenomenal hypocrisy had finally overridden any lingering thoughts of tolerance or forgiveness she might have entertained, and when, three decades ago tonight, they had checked into the Cottonwood Motel, she had come prepared for more than a night of love. She had let Buck shower, and, when he emerged, she had levelled the Smith and Wesson .38 at him, and blown a gaping hole in his chest. Then she'd run, throwing the gun away as she went, knowing the police were bound to catch her, and not much caring when they did. They'd taken her to Carson County Jail in Panhandle, and, after a few weeks, to trial. She never once tried to deny the murder: there'd been enough deception in her thirty-eight years of life as it was. And so, when they found her defiant, they took her to Huntsville State Prison, chose a bright day the following October, and summarily passed 2,250 volts through her body, stopping her unrepentant heart almost instantaneously. An eye for an eye; a tooth for a tooth. She had been brought up with such simple moral equations. She'd not been unhappy to die by the same mathematics.

But tonight she and Buck had elected to retrace the journey they'd taken thirty years before, to see if they could discover how and why their marriage had ended in murder. It was a chance offered to many dead lovers, though few, apparently, took it up; perhaps the thought of experiencing again the cataclysm that had ended their

103

lives was too distasteful. Sadie, however, couldn't help but wonder if it had all been predestined: if a tender word from Buck, or a look of genuine affection in his murky eyes, could have stayed her trigger finger and so saved both their lives. This one night stand would give them an opportunity to test history. Invisible, inaudible, they would follow the same route as they had three decades ago: the next few hours would tell if that route had led inevitably to murder.

Room Seven was occupied, and so was the room beside it; the interconnecting door was wide, and fluorescent lights burned in both. The occupancy was not a problem. Sadie had long become used to the ethereal state; to wandering unseen amongst the living. In such a condition she had attended her niece's wedding, and later on her father's funeral, standing beside the grave with the dead old man and gossiping about the mourners. Buck however – never an agile individual – was more prone to carelessness. She hoped he would be careful tonight. After all, he wanted to see the experiment through as much as she did.

As they stood on the threshold, and cast their eyes around the room in which their fatal farce had been played out, she wondered if the shot had hurt him very much. She must ask him tonight, she thought, should the opportunity arise.

There had been a young woman with a plain but pleasant face in the manager's office when Earl had gone in to book the rooms. She had now disappeared to be replaced by a man of sixty or so, wearing half a week's growth of mottled beard and a sweat-stained shirt. He looked up from a nose-close perusal of yesterday's *Pampa Daily News* when Earl entered.

'Yeah?'

'Is it possible to have some iced water?' Earl inquired. The man threw a hoarse yell over his shoulder: 'Laura-May? You in there?'

Through the doorway behind came the din of the late-night movie – shots, screams, the roar of an escaped beast – and then, Laura-May's response:

'What do you want, Pa?'

'There's a man wants room service,' Laura-May's father yelled back, not without a trace of irony in his voice. 'Will you get out here and serve him?'

No reply came; just more screams. They set Earl's teeth on edge. The manager glanced up at him. One of his eyes was clouded by a cataract.

'You with the evangelist?' he said.

'Yes . . . how did you know it was –?'

'Laura-May recognized him. Seen his picture in the paper.'

'That so?'

'Don't miss a trick, my baby.'

As if on cue Laura-May emerged from the room behind the office. When her brown eyes fell on Earl she visibly brightened.

'Oh . . .' she said, a smile quickening her features, 'what can I do for you, mister?' The line, coupled with the smile, seemed to signal more than polite interest in Earl; or was that just his wishful thinking? Except for a lady of the night he'd met in Pomca City, Oklahoma, his sex-life had been non-existent in the last three months. Taking his chance, he returned Laura-May's smile. Though she was at least thirty-five, her manner was curiously girlish; the look she was giving him almost intimidatingly direct. Meeting her eyes, Earl began to think that his first estimation had not been far off.

'Ice-water,' he said. 'I wondered if you had any? Mrs Gyer isn't feeling so well.'

Laura-May nodded. 'I'll get some,' she said, dallying for a moment in the door before returning into the television room. The din of the movie had abated – a scene of calm, perhaps, before the beast emerged again – and in the hush Earl could hear the rain beating down outside, turning the earth to mud.

'Quite a gully washer tonight, eh?' the manager observed, 'this keeps up, you'll be rained out tomorrow.'

'People come out in all kinds of weather,' Earl said, 'John Gyer's a big draw.'

The man pulled a face. 'Wouldn't rule out a tornado,' he said, clearly revelling in the role of doom-sayer. 'We're just about due for one.'

'Really?'

'Year before last, wind took the roof off the school. Just lifted it right off.'

Laura-May reappeared in the doorway with a tray on which a jug and four glasses were placed. Ice clinked against the jug's sides.

'What's that you say, Pa?' she asked.

'Tornado.'

'Isn't hot enough,' she announced with casual authority. Her father grunted his disagreement, but made no argument in return. Laura-May crossed towards Earl with the tray, but when he made a move to take it from her she said, 'I'll take it myself. You lead on.' He didn't object. It would give them a little while to exchange pleasantries as they walked to the Gyers' room; perhaps the same thought was in her mind. Either that, or she wanted a closer view of the evangelist.

They went together as far as the end of the office block walkway in silence; there they halted. Before them lay twenty yards of puddle-strewn earth between one building and the next.

'Shall I carry the jug?' Earl volunteered. 'You bring the glasses and the tray.'

106

'Sure,' she replied. Then, with the same direct look she'd given him before, she said: 'What's your name?'

'Earl,' he told her, 'Earl Rayburn.'

'I'm Laura-May Cade.'

'I'm most pleased to meet you, Laura-May.'

'You know about this place, do you?' she said. 'Papa told you, I suppose.'

'You mean the tornadoes?' he said.

'No,' she replied, 'I mean murder.'

Sadie stood at the bottom of the bed and looked at the woman lying on it. She had very little dress-sense, Sadie thought; the clothes were drab, and her hair wasn't fixed in a flattering way. She murmured something in her semi-comatose state, and then – abruptly – she woke. Her eyes opened wide. There was some unshaped alarm in them; and pain too. Sadie looked at her and sighed.

'What's the problem?' Buck wanted to know. He'd put down the cases and was sitting in a chair opposite the fourth occupant of the room, a large man with lean, forceful features and a mane of steel-grey hair that would not have shamed an Old Testament prophet.

'No problem,' Sadie replied.

'I don't want to share a room with these two,' Buck said.

'Well this is the room where . . . where we stayed,' Sadie replied.

'Let's move next door,' Buck suggested, nodding through the open door into Room Eight, 'we'll have more privacy.'

'They can't see us,' Sadie said.

'But I can see *them*,' Buck replied, 'and it gives me the creeps. It's not going to matter if we're in a different room, for Christ's sake.' Without waiting for agreement from Sadie, Buck picked up the cases and carried them through into Earl's room. 'Are you coming or not?' he asked Sadie. She nodded. It was better to give way to him; if she started to argue now they'd never get past the first hurdle. Conciliation was to be the key-note of this reunion, she reminded herself, and dutifully followed him into Room Eight.

On the bed, Virginia thought about getting up and going into the bathroom where, out of sight, she could take one or two tranquillizers. But John's presence frightened her; sometimes she felt he could see right into her, that all her private guilt was an open book to him. She was certain that if she got up now, and rooted in her bag for the medication, he would ask her what she was doing. If he did that, she'd blurt the truth out for certain. She didn't have the strength to resist the heat of his accusing eyes. No, it would be better to lie here and wait for Earl to come back with the water. Then, when the two men were discussing the tour, she would slip away to take the forbidden pills.

There was an evasive quality to the light in the room; it distressed her, and she wanted to close her lids against its tricks. Only moments before the light had conjured a mirage at the end of the bed; a moth-wing flicker of substance that had almost congealed in the air before flitting away.

Over by the window, John was again reading under his breath. At first, she caught only a few of the words –

'*And there came out of the smoke locusts upon the earth* . . .' She instantly recognized the passage; its imagery was unmistakable. '. . . *and unto them was given power, as the scorpions of the earth have power.*'

The verse was from The Revelations of St John the Divine. She knew the words that followed off by heart. He had declaimed them time after time at meetings.

'*And it was commanded them that they should not hurt the grass of the earth, neither any green thing, neither any tree; but only those men which have not the seal of God in their foreheads.*'

Gyer loved Revelations. He read it more often than the Gospels, whose stories he knew by heart but whose words did not ignite him the way the incantatory rhythms of Revelations did. When he preached Revelations, he shared the apocalyptic vision, and felt exulted by it. His voice would take on a different note; the poetry, instead of coming out of him, came *through* him. Helpless in its grip, he rose on a spiral of ever more awesome metaphor: from angels to dragons and thence to Babylon, the Mother of Harlots, sitting upon a scarlet-coloured beast.

Virginia tried to shut the words out. Usually, to hear her husband speak the poems of Revelations was a joy to her, but not tonight. Tonight the words seemed ripe to the point of corruption, and she sensed – perhaps for the first time – that he didn't really understand what he was saying; that the spirit of the words passed him by while he recited them. She made a small, unintentional noise of complaint. Gyer stopped reading.

'What is it?' he said.

She opened her eyes, embarrassed to have interrupted him.

'Nothing,' she said.

'Does my reading disturb you?' he wanted to know. The enquiry was a challenge, and she backed down from it.

'No,' she said. 'No, of course not.'

In the doorway between the two rooms, Sadie watched Virginia's face. The woman was lying of course; the words *did* disturb her. They disturbed Sadie too, but only because they seemed so pitifully melodramatic:

a drug–dream of Armageddon, more comical than intimidatory.

'Tell him,' she advised Virginia. '*Go on*. Tell him you don't like it.'

'Who are you talking to?' Buck said. 'They can't hear you.'

Sadie ignored her husband's remarks. 'Go on,' she said to Virginia, 'tell the bastard.'

But Virginia just lay there while Gyer took up the passage again, its absurdities escalating:

'*And the shapes of the locusts were unto horses prepared unto battle; and on their heads were as it were crowns like gold, and their faces were as the faces of men.*

'*And they had hair as the hair of women, and their teeth were as the teeth of lions.*'

Sadie shook her head: comic-book terrors, fit to scare children with. Why did people have to die to grow out of that kind of nonsense?

'Tell him,' she said again. 'Tell him how ridiculous he sounds.' Even as the words left her lips, Virginia sat up on the bed and said:

'John?'

Sadie stared at her, willing her on. 'Say it. *Say it.*'

'Do you have to talk about death all the time. It's very depressing.'

Sadie almost applauded; it wasn't quite the way *she* would have put it, but each to their own.

'What did you say?' Gyer asked her, assuming he'd heard incorrectly. Surely she wasn't challenging him?

Virginia put a trembling hand up to her lips, as if to cancel the words before they came again; but they came nevertheless.

'Those passages you read. I hate them. They're so . . .'

'Stupid,' Sadie prompted.

'. . . unpleasant,' Virginia said.

'Are you coming to bed or not?' Buck wanted to know.

'In a moment,' Sadie replied over her shoulder, 'I just want to see what happens in here.'

'Life isn't a soap-opera,' Buck chimed in. Sadie was about to beg to differ, but before she had a chance the evangelist had approached Virginia's bed, Bible in hand.

'This is the inspired word of the Lord, Virginia,' he said.

'I know John. But there are other passages . . .'

'I thought you liked the Apocalypse.'

'No,' she said, 'it distresses me.'

'You're tired,' he replied.

'Oh yes,' Sadie interjected, 'that's what they always tell you when you get too close to the truth. "You're tired," they say, "why don't you take a little nap?" '

'Why don't you sleep for a while?' Gyer said. 'I'll go next door and work.'

Virginia met her husband's condescending look for fully five seconds, then nodded.

'Yes,' she conceded, 'I *am* tired.'

'Foolish woman,' Sadie told her. 'Fight back, or he'll do the same again. Give them an inch and they take half the damn state.'

Buck appeared behind Sadie. 'I've asked you once,' he said, taking her arm, 'we're here to make friends. So let's get to it.' He pulled her away from the door, rather more roughly than was necessary. She shrugged off his hand.

'There's no need for violence, Buck,' she said.

'Ha! That's rich, coming from you,' Buck said with a humourless laugh. 'You want to see violence?' Sadie turned away from Virginia to look at her husband.

'*This* is violence,' he said. He had taken off his jacket; now he pulled his unbuttoned shirt open to reveal the shot-wound. At such close quarters Sadie's .38 had made a sizeable hole in Buck's chest, scorched and bloody: it was as fresh as the moment he died. He put his finger to it as if indicating the Sacred Heart. 'You see that, sweetheart mine? *You* made that.'

She peered at the hole with no little interest. It certainly was a permanent mark; about the only one she'd ever made on the man, she suspected.

'You cheated from the beginning, didn't you?' she said.

'We're not talking about cheating, we're talking about shooting,' Buck returned.

'Seems to me one subject leads to the other,' Sadie replied, 'And back again.'

Buck narrowed his already narrow eyes at her. Dozens of women had found that look irresistible, to judge by the numbers of anonymous mourners at his funeral. 'All right,' he said, 'I had women. So what?'

'So I shot you for it,' Sadie replied flatly. That was about all she had to say on the subject. It had made for a short trial.

'Well at least tell me you're sorry,' Buck burst out.

Sadie considered the proposition for a few moments and said: 'But I'm not!' She realized the response lacked tact, but it was the unavoidable truth. Even as they'd strapped her into the electric chair, with the priest doing his best to console her lawyer, she hadn't regretted the way things had turned out.

'This whole thing is useless,' Buck said. 'We came here to make peace and you can't even say you're sorry. You're a sick woman, you know that? You always were.

112

You pried into my business, you snooped around behind my back –'

'I did *not* snoop,' Sadie replied firmly. 'Your dirt came and found me.'

'Dirt?'

'Oh yes, Buck, *dirt*. It always was with you. Furtive and sweaty.'

He grabbed hold of her. 'Take that back!' he demanded.

'You used to frighten me once,' she replied, coolly. 'But then I bought a gun.'

He thrust her away from him. 'All right,' he said, 'don't say I didn't try. I wanted to see if we could forgive and forget; I really did. But you're not willing to give an inch are you?' He fingered his wound as he spoke, his voice softening. 'We could have had a good time here tonight, babe,' he murmured. 'Just you and me. I could have given you a bit of the old jazz, you know what I mean? Time was, you wouldn't have said no.'

She sighed softly. What he said was true. Time was she would have taken what little he gave her and counted herself a blessed woman. But times had changed.

'Come on, babe. Loosen up,' he said smokily, and began to unbutton his shirt completely, pulling it out of his trousers. His belly was bald as a baby's. 'What say we forget what you said and lie down and talk?'

She was about to reply to his suggestion when the door of Room Seven opened and in came the man with the soulful eyes, accompanied by a woman whose face rang a bell in Sadie's memory.

'Ice-water,' Earl said. Sadie watched him move across the room. There'd not been a man as fine as that in Wichita Falls; not that she could remember anyway. He almost made her want to live again.

113

'Are you going to get undressed?' Buck asked from the room behind her.

'In a minute, Buck. We've got all night, for Christ's sake.'

'I'm Laura-May Cade,' the woman with the familiar face said as she set the iced water down on the table.

Of course, thought Sadie, you're little Laura-May. The girl had been five or six when Sadie was last here: an odd, secretive child, full of sly looks. The intervening years had matured her physically, but the strangeness was still in evidence in her slightly off-centre features. Sadie turned to Buck, who was sitting on the bed untying his shoes.

'Remember the little girl?' she said, 'the one who you gave a quarter to, just to make her go away?'

'What about her?'

'She's here.'

'That so?' he replied, clearly uninterested.

Laura-May had poured the water, and was now taking the glass across to Virginia.

'It's real nice having you folks here,' she said. 'We don't get much happening here. Just the occasional tornado . . .'

Gyer nodded to Earl, who produced a five dollar bill and gave it to Laura-May. She thanked him, saying it wasn't necessary, then taking the bill. She wasn't to be bribed into leaving, however.

'This kind of weather makes people feel real peculiar,' she went on.

Earl could predict what subject was hovering behind Laura-May's lips. He'd already heard the bones of the story on the way across, and knew Virginia was in no mood to hear such a tale.

'Thank you for the water –' he said, putting a hand on Laura-May's arm to usher her through the door. But Gyer cut in.

114

'My wife's been suffering from heat exhaustion,' he said.

'You should be careful, ma'am,' Laura-May advised Virginia, 'people do some mighty weird things –'

'Like what?' Virginia asked.

'I don't think we –' Earl began, but before he could say – 'want to hear', Laura-May casually replied:

'Oh, murder mostly.'

Virginia looked up from the glass of iced-water in which her focus had been immersed.

'Murder?' she said.

'Hear that?' said Sadie, proudly. 'She remembers.'

'In this very room,' Laura-May managed to blurt before Earl forcibly escorted her out.

'Wait,' Virginia said as the two figures disappeared through the door. 'Earl! I want to hear what happened.'

'No you don't,' Gyer told her.

'Oh yes she does,' said Sadie very quietly, studying the look on Virginia's face. 'You'd *really* like to know, wouldn't you, Ginnie?'

For a moment pregnant with possibilities, Virginia looked away from the outside door and stared straight through into Room Eight, her eyes seeming to rest on Sadie. The look was so direct it could almost have been one of recognition. The ice in her glass tinkled. She frowned.

'What's wrong?' Gyer asked her.

Virginia shook her head.

'I asked you what was wrong,' Gyer insisted.

Virginia put down her glass on the bedside table. After a moment she said, very simply: 'There's somebody here, John.'

'What do you mean?'

'There's somebody in the room with us. I heard voices before. Raised voices.'

'Next door,' Gyer said.

'No, from Earl's room.'

'It's empty. It must have been next door.'

Virginia was not to be silenced with logic. 'I heard voices, I tell you. And I saw something at the end of the bed. Something in the air.'

'Oh my Jesus,' said Sadie, under her breath, 'the goddamn woman's psychic.'

Buck stood up. He was naked now, but for his shorts. He wandered over to the interconnecting door to look at Virginia with new appreciation.

'Are you sure?' he said.

'Hush,' Sadie told him, moving out of Virginia's eyeline. 'She said she could see us.'

'You're not well, Virginia,' Gyer was saying in the next room. 'It's those pills he fed you . . .'

'No,' Virginia replied, her voice rising. 'When will you stop talking about the pills? They were just to calm me down; help me sleep.'

She certainly wasn't calm now, thought Buck. He liked the way she trembled as she tried to hold back her tears. She looked in need of some of the old jazz, did poor Virginia; now *that* would help her sleep.

'I tell you I can see things,' she was telling her husband.

'That *I* can't –' Gyer replied, incredulously. 'Is that what you're saying? That you can see visions the rest of us are blind to?'

'I'm not proud of it, damn you,' she yelled at him, incensed by this inversion.

'Come away, Buck,' Sadie said. 'We're upsetting her. She knows we're here.'

'So what?' Buck responded. 'Her prick of a husband doesn't believe her. Look at him. He thinks she's crazy.'

'Well, we'll *make* her crazy if we parade around,' said Sadie. 'At least let's keep our voices down, huh?'

Buck looked around at Sadie, and offered up a dirty

rag of a smile. 'Want to make it worth my while?' he said sleazily. 'I'll keep out of the way if you and me can have some fun.'

Sadie hesitated a moment before replying. It was probably perverse to reject Buck's advances; the man was an emotional infant and always had been. Sex was one of the few ways he could express himself. 'All right, Buck,' she said, 'just let me freshen up and fix my hair.'

An uneasy truce had apparently been declared in Room Seven.

'I'm going to take a shower, Virginia,' Gyer said, 'I suggest you lie down and stop making a fool of yourself. You go talking like that in front of people and you'll jeopardize the crusade, you hear me?'

Virginia looked at her husband with clearer sight than she'd ever enjoyed before. 'Oh yes,' she said, without a trace of feeling in her voice, 'I hear you.'

He seemed satisfied. He slipped off his jacket and went into the bathroom, taking his Bible with him. She heard the door lock, and then exhaled a long, queasy sigh. There would be recriminations aplenty for the exchange they'd just had; he would squeeze every last drop of contrition from her in the days to come. She glanced around at the interconnecting door. There was no longer any sign of those shadows in the air; not the least whisper of lost voices. Perhaps, just *perhaps*, she had imagined it. She opened her bag and rummaged for the bottles of pills hidden there. One eye on the bathroom door, she selected a cocktail of three varieties and downed them with a gulp of iced-water. In fact, the ice in the jug had long since melted. The water she drank down was tepid, like the rain that fell relentlessly outside. By morning, perhaps the whole world would have been washed away. If it had, she mused, she wouldn't grieve.

'I asked you not to mention the killing,' Earl told Laura-May. 'Mrs Gyer can't take that kind of talk.'

'People are getting killed all the time,' Laura-May replied, unfazed. 'Can't go round with her head in a bucket.'

Earl said nothing. They had just got to the end of the walkway. The return sprint across the lot to the other building was ahead. Laura-May turned to face him. She was several inches the shorter of the two. Her eyes, turned up to his, were large and luminous. Angry as he was, he couldn't help but notice how full her mouth was, how her lips glistened.

'I'm sorry,' she said, 'I didn't mean to get you into trouble.'

'Sure I know. I'm just edgy.'

'It's the heat,' she returned. 'Like I said: puts thoughts into people's heads. You know.' Her look wavered for a moment; a hint of uncertainty crossed her face. Earl could feel the back of his neck tingle. This was his cue, wasn't it? she'd offered it unequivocally. But the words failed him. Finally, it was she who said:

'Do you have to go back there right now?'

He swallowed; his throat was dry. 'Don't see why,' he said, 'I mean, I don't want to get between them when they're having words with each other.'

'Bad blood?' she asked.

'I think so. I'm best leaving them to sort it out in peace. They don't want me.'

Laura-May looked down from Earl's face. 'Well I do,' she breathed, the words scarcely audible above the thump of the rain.

He put a cautious hand to her face and touched the down of her cheek. She trembled, ever so slightly. Then he bent his head to kiss her. She let him brush her lips with his.

'Why don't we go to my room?' she said against his mouth. 'I don't like it out here.'

'What about your Papa?'

'He'll be dead drunk by now; it's the same routine every night. Just take it quietly. He'll never know.'

Earl wasn't very happy with this game-plan. It was more than his job was worth to be found in bed with Laura-May. He was a married man, even if he hadn't seen Barbara in three months. Laura-May sensed his prevarication.

'Don't come if you don't want to,' she said.

'It's not that,' he replied.

As he looked down at her, she licked her lips. It was a completely unconscious motion, he felt sure, but it was enough to decide him. In a sense, though he couldn't know it at the time, all that lay ahead – the farce, the blood-letting, the inevitable tragedy – pivotted on Laura-May wetting her lower lip with such casual sensuality. 'Ah *shit*,' he said, 'you're too much, you know that?'

He bent to her and kissed her again, while somewhere over towards Skellytown the clouds gave out a loud roll of thunder, like a circus drummer before some particularly elaborate acrobatics.

In Room Seven, Virginia was having bad dreams. The pills had not secured her a safe harbour in sleep. Instead she'd been pitched into a howling tempest. In her dreams she was clinging to a crippled tree – a pitiful anchor in such a maelstrom – while the wind threw cattle and automobiles into the air, sucking half the world up into the pitch black clouds that boiled above her head. Just as she thought she must die here, utterly alone, she saw two figures a few yards from her, appearing and disappearing in the blinding veils of dust the wind was stirring up. She couldn't see their faces, so she called to them:

119

'Who are you?'

Next door, Sadie heard Virginia talking in her sleep. What was the woman dreaming about? she wondered. She fought the temptation to go next door and whisper in the dreamer's ear, however.

Behind Virginia's eyelids the dream raged on. Though she called to the strangers in the storm they seemed not to hear her. Rather than be left alone, she forsook the comfort of the tree – which was instantly uprooted and whirled away – and battled through the biting dust to where the strangers stood. As she approached, a sudden lull in the wind revealed them to her. One was male, the other female: both were armed. As she called to them to make herself known they attacked each other, opening fatal wounds in neck and torso.

'Murder!' she shouted as the wind spattered her face with the antagonists' blood. 'For God's sake, somebody stop them! Murder!'

And suddenly she was awake, her heart beating fit to burst. The dream still flitted behind her eyes. She shook her head to rid herself of the horrid images, then moved groggily to the edge of the bed and stood up. Her head felt so light it might float off like a balloon. She needed some fresh air. Seldom in her life had she felt so strange. It was as though she was losing her slender grip on what was real; as though the solid world were slipping through her fingers. She crossed to the outside door. In the bathroom she could hear John, speaking aloud: addressing the mirror, no doubt, to refine every detail of his delivery. She stepped out onto the walkway. There was some refreshment to be had out here, but precious little. In one of the rooms at the end of the block a child was crying. As she listened a sharp voice silenced it. For maybe ten seconds the voice was hushed; then it began again in a higher key. *Go on*, she told the child, *you cry; there's plenty of reason*. She trusted unhappiness in people; more and more it was *all* she trusted. Sadness was so much more honest than the artificial bonhomie that was all the style these days: that façade of empty-headed optimism that was plastered over the despair that everyone felt in their heart of hearts. The child was expressing that wise panic now, as it cried in the night. She silently applauded its honesty.

In the bathroom, John Gyer tired of the sight of his own face in the mirror, and gave some time over to thought. He put down the toilet lid and sat in silence for several minutes. He could smell his own stale sweat; he needed a shower, and then a good night's sleep. Tomorrow: Pampa. Meetings, speeches; thousands of hands to be shaken and blessings to be bestowed. Sometimes he felt so tired: and then he'd get to wondering if the Lord couldn't lighten his burden a little. But that was the Devil talking in his ear, wasn't it? He knew better than to pay that scurrilous voice much attention. If you listened *once* the doubts would get a hold, the way they had of Virginia. Somewhere along the road, while his back had been turned about the Lord's business, she'd lost her way, and the Old One had found her wandering. He, John Gyer, would have to bring her back to the path of the righteous; make her see the danger her soul was in. There would be tears and complaints; maybe she would be bruised a little. But bruises healed.

He put down his Bible, and went down on his knees in the narrow space between the bath and the towel rack, and began to pray. He tried to find some benign words, a gentle prayer to ask for the strength to finish his task, and to bring Virginia back to her senses. But mildness had deserted him. It was the vocabulary of Revelations that came back to his lips, unbidden. He let the words spill out, even though the fever in him burned brighter with every syllable he spoke.

121

'What do you think?' Laura-May had asked Earl as she escorted him into her bedroom. Earl was too startled by what was in front of him to offer any coherent reply. The bedroom was a mausoleum, founded, it seemed, in the name of Trivia. Laid out on the shelves, hung on the walls and covering much of the floor were items that might have been picked off any rubbish tip: empty Coke cans, collections of ticket stubs, coverless and defaced magazines, vandalized toys, shattered mirrors, postcards never sent, letters never read – a limping parade of the forgotten and the forsaken. His eye passed back and forth over the elaborate display and found not one item of worth amongst the junk and bric-a-brac. Yet all this inconsequentia had been arranged with meticulous care, so that no one piece masked another; and – now that he looked more closely – he saw that every item was numbered, as if each had its place in some system of junk. The thought that this was all Laura-May's doing shrank Earl's stomach. The woman was clearly verging on lunacy.

'This is my collection,' she told him.

'So I see,' he replied.

'I've been collecting since I was six.' She crossed the room to the dressing table, where most women Earl had known would have arranged their toiletries. But here were arrayed more of the same inane exhibits. 'Everybody leaves something behind, you know,' Laura-May said to Earl, picking up some piece of dreck with all the care others might bestow on a precious stone, and examining it before placing it back in its elected position.

'Is that so?' Earl said.

'Oh yeah. Everyone. Even if it's only a dead match or a tissue with lipstick on. We used to have a Mexican girl, Ophelia, who cleaned the rooms when I was a child.

122

It started as a game with her, really. She'd always bring me something belonging to the guests who'd left. When she died I took over collecting stuff for myself, always keeping something. As a memento.'

Earl began to grasp the absurd poetry of the museum. In Laura-May's neat body was all the ambition of a great curator. Not for her mere *art*; she was collecting keepsakes of a more intimate nature, forgotten signs of people who'd passed this way, and who, most likely, she would never see again.

'You've got it all marked,' he observed.

'Oh yes,' she replied, 'it wouldn't be much use if I didn't know who it all belonged to, would it?'

Earl supposed not. 'Incredible,' he murmured, quite genuinely. She smiled at him; he suspected she didn't show her collection to many people. He felt oddly honoured to be viewing it.

'I've got some really prize things,' she said, opening the middle drawer of the dressing table, 'stuff I don't put on display.'

'Oh?' he said.

The drawer she'd opened was lined with tissue paper, which rustled as she brought forth a selection of special acquisitions. A soiled tissue found beneath the bed of a Hollywood star who had tragically died six weeks after staying at the Motel. A heroin needle carelessly left by X; an empty book of matches, which she had traced to a homosexual bar in Amarillo, discarded by Y. The names she mentioned meant little or nothing to Earl, but he played the game as he felt she wanted it played, mingling exclamations of disbelief with gentle laughter. Her pleasure, fed by his, grew. She took him through all the exhibits in the dressing-table drawer, offering some anecdote or biographical insight with every one. When she had finished, she said:

'I wasn't quite telling you the truth before, when I

said it began as a game with Ophelia. That really came later.'

'So what started you off?' he asked.

She went down on her haunches and unlocked the bottom drawer of the dressing-table with a key on a chain around her neck. There was only one artifact in this drawer; this she lifted out almost reverentially, and stood up to show him.

'What's this?'

'You asked me what started the collection,' she said. 'This is it. I found it, and I never gave it back. You can look if you want.'

She extended the prize towards him, and he unfolded the pressed white cloth the object had been wrapped up in. It was a gun. A Smith and Wesson .38, in pristine condition. It took him only a moment to realize which motel guest this piece of history had once belonged to.

'The gun that Sadie Durning used . . .' he said, picking it up. 'Am I right?'

She beamed. 'I found it in the scrub behind the motel, before the police got to searching for it. There was such a commotion, you know, nobody looked twice at me. And of course they didn't try and look for it in the light.'

'Why was that?'

'The '55 tornado hit, just the day after. Took the motel roof right off; blew the school away. People were killed that year. We had funerals for weeks.'

'They didn't question you at all?'

'I was a good liar,' she replied, with no small satisfaction.

'And you never owned up to having it? All these years?'

She looked faintly contemptuous of the suggestion. 'They might have taken it off me,' she said.

'But it's *evidence*.'

'They executed her anyway, didn't they?' she replied. Sadie admitted to it all, right from the beginning. It wouldn't have made any difference if they'd found the murder-weapon or not.'

Earl turned the gun over in his hand. There was incrusted dirt on it.

'That's blood,' Laura-May informed him. 'It was still wet when I found it. She must have touched Buck's body, to make sure he was dead. Only used two bullets. The rest are still in there.'

Earl had never much liked weapons, since his brother-in-law had blown off three of his toes in an accident. The thought that the .38 was still loaded made him yet more apprehensive. He put it back in its wrapping, and folded the cloth over it.

'I've never seen anything like this place,' he said as Laura-May knelt to return the gun to the drawer. 'You're quite a woman, you know that?'

She looked up at him. Her hand slowly slid up the front of his trousers.

'I'm glad you like what you see,' she said.

'Sadie . . .? Are you coming to bed or not?'

'I just want to finish fixing my hair.'

'You're not playing fair. Forget your hair and come over here.'

'In a minute.'

'Shit!'

'You're in no hurry, are you, Buck? I mean, you're not going anywhere?'

She caught his reflection in the mirror. He gave her a sour glance.

'You think it's funny, don't you?' he said.

'Think *what's* funny?'

'What happened. Me getting shot. You getting the hair. It gives you some perverse satisfaction.'

She thought about this for a few moments. It was the first time Buck had shown any real desire to talk seriously; she wanted to answer with the truth.

'Yes,' she said, when she was certain that was the answer. 'Yes; I suppose it did please me, in an odd sort of way.'

'I *knew* it,' said Buck.

'Keep your voice down,' Sadie snapped, 'she'll hear us.'

'She's gone outside. I heard her. And don't change the subject.' He rolled over and sat on the edge of the bed. the wound did look painful, Sadie thought.

'Did it hurt much?' she asked, turning to him.

'Are you kidding?' he said, displaying the hole for her. 'What does it fucking look like?'

'I thought it would be quick. I never wanted you to suffer.'

'Is that right?' Buck said.

'Of course. I loved you once, Buck. I really did. You know what the headline was the day after?'

'No', Buck replied, 'I was otherwise engaged, remember?'

' "*Motel Becomes Slaughter-house of Love*",' it said. There were pictures of the room; of the blood on the floor; and you being carried out under a sheet.'

'My finest hour,' he said bitterly. 'And I don't even get my face in the press.'

'I'll never forget the phrase. "*Slaughter-house of Love!*" I thought it was romantic. Don't you?' Buck grunted in disgust. Sadie went on anyway. 'I got three hundred proposals of marriage while I was waiting for the chair did I ever tell you that?'

'Oh yeah?' Buck said. 'Did they come and visit you? Give you a bit of the old jazz to keep your mind off the big day?'

'No,' said Sadie frostily.

'You could have had a time of it. I would have done.'

'I'm sure you would,' she replied.

'Just thinking about it's getting me cooking, Sadie. Why don't you come and get it while it's hot?'

'We came here to talk, Buck.'

'We talked, for Christ's sake,' he said, 'I don't want to talk no more. Now come here. You promised.' He rubbed his abdomen, and gave her a crooked smile. 'Sorry about the blood and all, but I ain't responsible for that.'

Sadie stood up.

'Now you're being sensible,' he said.

As Sadie Durning crossed to the bed, Virginia came in out of the rain. It had cooled her face somewhat, and the tranquillisers she'd taken were finally beginning to soothe her system. In the bathroom, John was still praying, his voice rising and falling. She crossed to the table and glanced at his notes, but the tightly packed words wouldn't come into focus. She picked the papers up to peer more closely at them; as she did so she heard a groan from the next room. She froze. The groan came again, more loudly. The papers trembled in her hands; she made to put them back on the table but the voice came a third time, and this time the papers slipped from her hand.

'Give a little, damn you . . .' the voice said; the words, though blurred, were unmistakable; more grunts followed. Virginia moved towards the door between the rooms, the trembling spreading up from her hands to the rest of her body. 'Play the game, will you?' the voice came again; there was anger in it. Cautiously Virginia looked through into Room Eight, holding onto the door lintel for support. There was a shadow on the bed; it writhed distressingly, as if attempting to devour itself. She stood, rooted to the spot, trying to stifle a cry, while more sounds rose from the shadow. Not *one* voice this time, but two. The words were jumbled; in her growing panic she could make little sense of them. She couldn't turn her back on the scene, however. She stared on, trying to make some sense of the shifting configuration. Now a smattering of words came clear; and with them, a recognition of the event on the bed. She heard a woman's voice, protesting; now she even began to see the speaker, struggling beneath a partner who was attempting to arrest her flailing arms. Her first instincts about the scene had been correct: it *was* a devouring, of a kind.

Sadie looked up into Buck's face. That bastard grin of his had returned; it made her trigger-finger itch. This is what he'd come for tonight. Not for conversation about failed dreams: but to humiliate her the way he had so often in the past, whispering obscenities into her neck while he pinned her to the sheets. The pleasure he took in her discomfort made her seethe.

'*Let go of me!*' she shouted, louder than she'd intended.

At the door, Virginia said: 'Let her alone.'

'We've got an audience,' Buck Durning grinned, pleased by the appalled look on Virginia's face. Sadie took advantage of his diverted attention. She slipped her arm from his grasp and pushed him off her; he rolled off the narrow bed with a yell. As she stood up, she looked round at the ashen woman in the doorway; how much could Virginia see or hear? Enough to know who they were?

Buck was climbing over the bed towards his sometime murderer. 'Come on,' he said, 'it's only the crazy lady.'

'Keep away from me,' Sadie warned.

'You can't harm me now, woman. I'm already dead, remember?' His exertions had opened the gun-shot wound. There was blood smeared all over him; over her too, now she looked. She backed towards the door. There was nothing to be salvaged here. What little chance of reconciliation there had been had degenerated into a bloody farce. The only solution to the whole sorry mess was to get out, and leave poor Virginia to make what sense of it she could. The longer she stayed to fight with Buck, the worse the situation would become for all three of them.

'Where are you going?' Buck demanded.

'Out,' she responded. 'Away from you. I said I loved you, Buck, didn't I? Well . . . maybe I did. But I'm cured now.'

'Bitch!'

'Goodbye Buck. Have a nice eternity.'

'*Worthless bitch!*'

She didn't reply to his insults; she simply walked through the door and out into the night.

Virginia watched the shadow pass through the closed door and held on to the tattered remains of her sanity with white-knuckled fists. She had to put these apparitions out of her head as quickly as possible, or she knew she'd go crazy. She turned her back on Room Eight. What she needed now was pills. She picked up her handbag, only to drop it again as her shaking fingers rooted for the bottles, depositing the contents of the bag on to the floor. One of the bottles, which she had failed to seal properly, spilled. A rainbow assortment of tablets rolled across the stained carpet in every direction. She bent to pick them up. Tears had started to come, blinding her; she felt for the pills as best she could, feeding half a handful into her mouth and trying to swallow them dry. The tattoo of the rain on the roof sounded louder and louder in her head; a roll of thunder gave weight to the percussion.

And then, John's voice:

'*What are you doing, Virginia?*'

She looked up, tears in her eyes, a pill-laden hand hovering at her lips. She'd forgotten her husband entirely; the shadows and the rain and the voices had driven all thought of him from her head. She let the pills drop back to the carpet. Her limbs were shaking; she hadn't got the strength to stand up.

'I . . . I . . . heard the voices again,' she said.

His eyes had come to rest on the spilled contents of bag and bottle. Her crime was spread for him to see quite plainly. It was useless to try and deny anything; it would only enrage him further.

'Woman,' he said. 'Haven't you learned your lesson?'

She didn't reply. Thunder drowned his next words. He repeated them, more loudly.

'Where did you get the pills, Virginia?'

She shook her head, weakly.

'Earl again, I suppose. Who else?'

'No,' she murmured.

'Don't lie to me, Virginia!' He had raised his voice to compete with the storm. 'You know the Lord hears your lies, as I hear them. And you are *judged*, Virginia! *Judged!*'

'Please leave me be,' she pleaded.

'You're poisoning yourself.'

'I *need* them, John,' she told him, 'I really do.' She had no energy to hold his bullying at bay; nor did she want him to take the pills from her. But then what was the use of protesting? He would have his way, as always. It would be wiser to give up the booty now, and save herself unnecessary anguish.

'Look at yourself,' he said, 'grovelling on the floor.'

'Don't start on me, John,' she replied. 'You win. Take the pills. Go on! *Take them!*'

He was clearly disappointed by her rapid capitulation, like an actor preparing for a favourite scene only to find the curtain rung down prematurely. But he made the most of her invitation, upending her handbag on the bed, and collecting the bottles.

130

'Is this all?' he demanded.

'Yes,' she said.

'I won't be deceived, Virginia.'

'*That's all!*' she shouted back at him. Then more softly: 'I swear . . . that's all.'

'Earl will be sorry. I promise you that. He's exploited your weakness –'

'. . . no!'

'– your weakness and your fear. The man is in Satan's employ, that much is apparent.'

'Don't talk rubbish!' she said, surprising herself with her own vehemence. 'I *asked* him to supply them.' She got to her feet with some difficulty. 'He didn't want to defy you, John. It was me all along.'

Gyer shook his head. 'No, Virginia. You won't save him. Not this time. He's worked to subvert me all along. I see that now. Worked to harm my crusade through you. Well I'm wise to him now. Oh yes. Oh *yes*.'

He suddenly turned and pitched the handful of bottles through the open door and into the rainy darkness outside. Virginia watched them fly, and felt her heart sink. There was precious little sanity to be had on a night like this – it was a night for going crazy, wasn't it?, with the rain bruising your skull and murder in the air – and now the damn fool had thrown away her last chance of equilibrium. He turned back to her, his perfect teeth bared.

'How many times do you have to be told?'

He was not to be denied his scene after all, it seemed.

'I'm not listening!' she told him, clamping her hands over her ears. Even so she could hear the rain. 'I *won't* listen!'

'I'm patient, Virginia,' he said. 'The Lord will have his Judgement in the fullness of time. Now, where's Earl?'

She shook her head. Thunder came again; she wasn't sure if it was inside or out.

'*Where is he?*' he boomed at her. 'Gone for more of the same filth?'

'No!' she yelled back. 'I don't know where he's gone.'

'You pray, woman,' Gyer said. 'You get down on your knees and thank the Lord I'm here to keep you from Satan.'

Content that his words made a striking exit-line, he headed out in search of Earl, leaving Virginia shaking, but curiously elated. He would be back, of course. There would be more recriminations, and from her, the obligatory tears. As to Earl, he would have to defend himself as best he could. She slumped down on the bed, and her bleary eyes came to rest on the tablets that were still scattered across the floor. All was not quite lost. There were no more than two dozen, so she would have to be sparing in her use of them, but they were better than nothing at all. Wiping her eyes with the back of her hands, she knelt down again to gather the pills up. As she did so she realized that someone had their eyes on her. Not the evangelist, back so soon? She looked up. The door out to the rain was still wide open, but he wasn't standing there. Her heart seemed to lose its rhythm for a moment, as she remembered the shadows in the room next door. There had been *two*. One had departed; but the other —?

Her eyes slid across to the interconnecting door. It was there, a greasy smudge that had taken on a new solidity since last she'd set eyes on it. Was it that the apparition was gaining coherence, or that she was seeing it in more detail? It was quite clearly human; and just as apparently male. It was staring at her, she had no doubt of that. She could even see its eyes, when she concentrated. Her tenuous grasp of its existence was improving; it was gaining fresh resolution with every trembling breath she took.

She stood up, very slowly. It took a step through the interconnecting door. She moved toward the outside door, and it matched her move with one of its own, sliding with eerie speed between her and the night. Her outstretched arm brushed against its smoky form, and, as if illuminated by a lightning flash, an entire portrait of her accoster sprang into view in front of her, only to disappear as she withdrew her hand. She had glimpsed enough to appal her, however. The vision was that of a dead man; his chest had been blown open. Was this more of her dream, spilling into the living world? She thought of calling after John, to summon him back, but that meant approaching the door again, and risking contact with the apparition. Instead she took a cautious step backwards, reciting a prayer beneath her breath as she did so. Perhaps John had been correct all along; perhaps she *had* invited this lunacy on to herself with the very tablets she was even now treading to powder underfoot. The apparition closed in on her. Was it her imagination, or had it opened its arms, as if to embrace her?

Her heel caught on the skirt of the coverlet. Before she could stop herself she was toppling backwards. Her arms flailed, seeking support. Again she made contact with the dream-thing; again the whole horrid picture appeared in front of her. But this time it didn't disappear, because the apparition had snatched at her hand and was grasping it tight. Her fingers felt as though they'd been plunged into ice-water. She yelled for it to let her be, flinging up her free arm to push her assailant away, but it simply grasped her other hand too.

Unable to resist, she met its gaze. They were not the Devil's eyes that looked at her – they were slightly stupid, even comical, eyes – and below them a weak mouth which only reinforced her impression of witlessness. Suddenly she was not afraid. This was no demon. It was a delusion, brought on by exhaustion and pills; it could do her no harm. The only danger here was that she hurt herself in her attempts to keep the hallucinations at bay.

Buck sensed that Virginia was losing the will to resist. 'That's better,' he coaxed her. 'You just want a bit of the old jazz, don't you, Ginnie?'

He wasn't certain if she heard him, but no matter. He could readily make his intentions apparent. Dropping one of her hands, he ran his palm across her breasts. She sighed, a bewildered expression in her beautiful eyes, but she made no effort to resist his attentions.

'You don't exist,' she told him plainly. 'You're only in my mind, like John said. The pills made you. The pills did it all.'

Buck let the woman babble; let her think whatever she pleased, as long as it made her compliant.

'That's right, isn't it?' she said. 'You're not real, are you?'

He obliged her with a polite reply. 'Certainly,' he said, squeezing her. 'I'm just a dream, that's all.' The answer seemed to satisfy her. 'No need to fight me is there?' he said. 'I'll have come and gone before you know it.'

The manager's office lay empty. From the room beyond it, Gyer heard a television. It stood to reason that Earl must be somewhere in the vicinity. He had left their room with the girl who'd brought the iced-water, and they certainly wouldn't be taking a walk together in weather like this. The thunder had moved in closer in the last few minutes. Now it was almost overhead. Gyer enjoyed the noise, and the spectacle of the lightning. It fuelled his sense of occasion.

'Earl!' he yelled, making his way through the office and into the room with the television. The late movie was nearing its climax, the sound turned up deafeningly loud. A fantastical beast of some kind was treading Tokyo to rubble; citizens fled, screaming. Asleep in a chair in front of this papier-mâché Apocalypse was a late middle-aged man. Neither the thunder nor Gyer's calls had stirred him. A tumbler of spirits, nursed in his lap, had slipped from his hand and stained his trousers. The whole scene stank of bourbon and depravity; Gyer made a note of it for future use in the pulpit.

A chill blew in from the office. Gyer turned, expecting a visitor, but there was nobody in the office behind him. He stared into space. All the way across here he'd had a sense of being followed, yet there was nobody on his heels. He cancelled his suspicions. Fears like this were for women and old men, afraid of the dark. He stepped between the sleeping drunkard and the ruin of Tokyo toward the closed door beyond.

'Earl?' he called out, 'answer me!'

Sadie watched Gyer open the door and step into the kitchen. His bombast amazed her. She'd expected his sub-species to be extinct by now: could such melodrama be credible in this sophisticated age? She'd never much liked church people, but this example was particularly offensive; there was more than a whiff of malice beneath the flatulence. He was riled and unpredictable, and he would not be pleased by the scene that awaited him in Laura-May's room. Sadie had already been there. She had watched the lovers for a little time, until their passion became too much for her and had driven her out to cool herself by watching the rain. Now the evangelist's appearance drew her back the way she'd come, fearful that whatever was now in the air, the night's events could not end well. In the kitchen, Gyer was shouting again. He clearly enjoyed the sound of his own voice.

'Earl! You hear me? I'm not to be cheated!'

In Laura-May's room Earl was attempting to perform three acts at the same time. One, kiss the woman he had just made love with; two, pull on his damp trousers; and three, invent an adequate excuse to offer Gyer if the evangelist reached the bedroom door before some illusion of innocence had been created. As it was, he had no time to complete any of the tasks. His tongue was still locked in Laura-May's tender mouth when the lock on the door was forced.

'Found you!'

Earl broke his kiss and turned towards the messianic voice. Gyer was standing in the doorway, rain-plastered hair a grey skull cap, his face bright with fury. The light thrown up on him from the silk-draped lamp beside the bed made him look massive; the glint in his come-to-the-Lord eyes was verging on the manic. Earl had heard tell of the great man's righteous wrath from Virginia: furniture had been trashed in the past, and bones broken.

'Is there no end to your iniquity?' he demanded to know, the words coming with unnerving calm from between his narrow lips. Earl hoisted his trousers up, fumbling for the zip.

'This isn't your business . . .' he began, but Gyer's fury powdered the words on his tongue.

Laura-May was not so easily cowed. 'You get out,' she said, pulling a sheet up to cover her generous breasts. Earl glanced round at her; at the smooth shoulders he'd all too recently kissed. He wanted to kiss them again now, but the man in black crossed the room in four quick strides and took hold of him by hair and arm. The movement, in the confined space of Laura-May's room, had the effect of an earth tremor. Pieces of her precious collection toppled over on the shelves and dressing-table, one exhibit falling against another, and that against its neighbour, until a minor avalanche of trivia hit the

136

floor. Laura-May was blind to any damage however; her thoughts were with the man who had so sweetly shared her bed. She could see the trepidation in Earl's eyes as the evangelist dragged him away, and she shared it.

'Let him be!' she shrieked, forsaking her modesty and getting up from the bed. 'He hasn't done anything wrong!'

The evangelist paused to respond, Earl wrestling uselessly to free himself. 'What would you know about error, *whore*?' Gyer spat at her, 'You're too steeped in sin. You with your nakedness and your stinking bed.'

The bed did stink, but only of good soap and recent love. She had nothing to apologize for, and she wasn't going to let this two-bit Bible-thumper intimidate her.

'I'll call the cops!' she warned. 'If you don't leave him alone, I'll call them!'

Gyer didn't grace the threat with a reply. He simply dragged Earl out through the door and into the kitchen. Laura-May yelled: 'Hold on, Earl. I'll get help!' Her lover didn't answer; he was too busy preventing Gyer from pulling out his hair by the roots.

Sometimes, when the days were long and lonely, Laura-May had day-dreamed dark men like the evangelist. She had imagined them coming before tornadoes, wreathed in dust. She had pictured herself lifted up by them – only half against her will – and taken away. But the man who had lain in her bed tonight had been utterly unlike her fever-dream lovers; he had been foolish and vulnerable. If he were to die at the hands of a man like Gyer – whose image she had conjured in her desperation – she would never forgive herself.

She heard her father say: 'What's going on?' in the far room. Something fell and smashed; a plate perhaps, from off the dresser, or a glass from his lap. She prayed her Papa wouldn't try and tackle the evangelist: he would be chaff in the wind if he did. She went back to the bed to root for her clothes; they were wound up in the sheets, and her frustration mounted with every second she lost searching for them. She tossed the pillows aside. One landed on the dressing table; more of her exquisitely arranged pieces were swept to the floor. As she pulled on her underwear her father appeared at the door. His drink-flushed features turned a deeper red seeing her state.

'What you been doing, Laura-May?'

'Never mind, Pa. There's no time to explain.'

'But there's men out there –'

'I know. I know. I want you to call the Sheriff in Panhandle. Understand?'

'What's going on?'

'Never mind. Just call Alvin and be quick about it, or we're going to have another murder on our hands.'

The thought of slaughter galvanized Milton Cade. He disappeared, leaving his daughter to finish dressing. Laura-May knew that on a night like this Alvin Baker and his Deputy could be a long time coming. In the meanwhile God alone knew what the mad-dog preacher would be capable of.

From the doorway, Sadie watched the woman dress. Laura-May was a plain creature, at least to Sadie's critical eye, and her fair skin made her look wan and insubstantial, despite her full figure. But then, thought Sadie, who am I to complain of lack of substance? Look at me. And for the first time in the thirty years since her death she felt a nostalgia for corporeality. In part because she envied Laura-May her bliss with Earl, and in part because she itched to have a role in the drama that was rapidly unfolding around her.

In the kitchen an abruptly sobered Milton Cade was blabbering on the phone, trying to rouse some action from the people in Panhandle, while Laura-May, who had finished dressing, unlocked the bottom drawer of her dressing-table and rummaged for something. Sadie peered over the woman's shoulder to discover what the trophy was, and a thrill of recognition made her scalp tingle as her eyes alighted on her .38. So it was Laura-May who had found the gun; the whey-faced six-year-old who had been running up and down the walkway all that evening thirty years ago, playing games with herself and singing songs in the hot still air.

It delighted Sadie to see the murder-weapon again. Maybe, she thought I *have* left some sign of myself to help shape the future; maybe I *am* more than a headline on a yellowed newspaper, and a dimming memory in ageing heads. She watched with new and eager eyes as Laura-May slipped on some shoes and headed out into the bellowing storm.

Virginia sat slumped against the wall of Room Seven, and looked across at the seedy figure leaning on the door-lintel across from her. She had let the delusion she had conjured have what way it would with her; and never in her forty-odd years had she heard such depravity promised. But though the shadow had come at her again and again, pressing its cold body on to hers, its icy, slack mouth against her own, it had failed to carry one act of violation through. Three times it had tried; three times the urgent words whispered in her ear had not been realized. Now it guarded the door, preparing, she guessed, for a further assault. Its face was clear enough for her to read the bafflement and the shame in its features. It viewed her, she thought, with murder on its mind.

Outside, she heard her husband's voice above the din of the thunder, and Earl's voice too, raised in protest. There was a fierce argument going on, that much was apparent. She slid up the wall, trying to make out the words; the delusion watched her balefully.

139

'You failed,' she told it.

It didn't reply.

'You're just a dream of mine; and you failed.'

It opened its mouth and waggled its pallid tongue. She didn't understand why it hadn't evaporated; but perhaps it would tag along with her until the pills had worked their way through her system. No matter. She had endured the worst it could offer; now, given time, it would surely leave her be. Its failed rapes left it bereft of power over her.

She crossed towards the door, no longer afraid. It raised itself from its slouched posture.

'Where are you going?' it demanded.

'Out,' she said. 'To help Earl.'

'No,' it told her, 'I haven't finished with you.'

'You're just a phantom,' she retorted. 'You can't stop me.'

It offered up a grin that was three parts malice to one part charm. 'You're wrong, Virginia,' Buck said. There was no purpose in deceiving the woman any longer; he'd tired of that particular game. And perhaps he'd failed to get the old jazz going because she'd given herself to him so easily, believing he was some harmless nightmare. 'I'm no delusion, woman,' he said, '*I'm Buck Durning.*' She frowned at the wavering figure. Was this a new trick her psyche was playing? 'Thirty years ago I was shot dead in this very room. Just about where you're standing in fact.'

Instinctively, Virginia glanced down at the carpet at her feet, almost expecting the blood-stains to be still there.

'We came back tonight, Sadie and I,' the ghost went on. 'A one-night-stand at the Slaughterhouse of Love. That's what they called this place, did you know that? People used to come here from all over, just to peer in at this very room; just to see where Sadie Durning had shot her husband Buck. Sick people, Virginia, don't you think? More interested in murder than love. Not me . . . I've always liked love, you know? Almost the only thing I've ever had much of a talent for, in fact.'

'You lied to me,' she said. 'You *used* me.'

'I haven't finished yet,' Buck promised. 'In fact I've barely started.'

He moved from the door towards her, but she was prepared for him this time. As he touched her, and the smoke was made flesh again, she threw a blow towards him. Buck moved to avoid it, and she dodged past him towards the door. Her untied hair got in her eyes, but she virtually threw herself towards freedom. A cloudy hand snatched at her, but the grasp was too tenuous, and slipped.

'I'll be waiting,' Buck called after her as she stumbled across the walkway and into the storm. 'You hear me, bitch? *I'll be waiting*!'

He wasn't going to humiliate himself with a pursuit. She would have to come back, wouldn't she? And he, invisible to all but the woman, could afford to bide his time. If she told her companions what she'd seen, they'd call her crazy; maybe lock her up where he could have her all to himself. No, he had a winner here. She would return soaked to the skin, her dress clinging to her in a dozen fetching ways; panicky perhaps; tearful; too weak to resist his overtures. They'd make music then. Oh yes. Until she begged him to stop.

Sadie followed Laura-May out.

'Where are you going?' Milton asked his daughter, but she didn't reply. 'Jesus!' he shouted after her, registering what he'd seen. 'Where'd you get the goddamn gun?'

The rain was torrential; it beat on the ground, on the last leaves of the cottonwood, on the roof, on the skull. It

141

flattened Laura-May's hair in seconds, pasting it to her forehead and neck.

'Earl?' she yelled. 'Where are you? *Earl*?' She began to run across the lot, yelling his name as she went. The rain had turned the dust to a deep brown mud; it slopped up against her shins. She crossed to the other building. A number of guests, already woken by Gyer's barrage, watched her from their windows. Several doors were open; one man, standing on the walkway with a beer in his hand, demanded to know what was going on. 'People running around like crazies,' he said. 'All this yelling. 'We came here for some privacy, for Christ's sake.' A girl – fully twenty years his junior – emerged from the room behind the beer-drinker. 'She's got a gun, Dwayne,' she said. 'See that?'

'Where did they go?' Laura-May asked the beer-drinker.

'Who?' Dwayne replied.

'*The crazies!*' Laura-May yelled back, above another peal of thunder.

'They went round the back of the office,' Dwayne said, his eyes on the gun rather than Laura-May. 'They're not here. Really they're not.'

Laura-May doubled back towards the office building. The rain and lightning were blinding, and she had difficulty keeping her balance in the swamp underfoot.

'Earl!' she called. 'Are you there?'

Sadie kept pace with her. The Cade woman had pluck, no doubt of that, but there was an edge of hysteria in her voice which Sadie didn't like too much. This kind of business (murder) required detachment. The trick was to do it almost casually, as you might flick on the radio, or swat a mosquito. Panic would only cloud the issue; passion the same. Why, when she'd raised that .38 and pointed it at Buck there'd been no anger to spoil her aim, not a trace. In the final analysis, that

142

was why they'd sent her to the chair. Not for doing it, but for doing it too well.

Laura-May was not so cool. Her breath had become ragged, and from the way she sobbed Earl's name as she ran it was clear she was close to breaking-point. She rounded the back of the office building, where the motel sign threw a cold light on the waste ground, and this time, when she called for Earl, there *was* an answering cry. She stopped, peering through the veil of rain. It was Earl's voice, as she'd hoped, but he wasn't calling to her.

'Bastard!' he was yelling, 'you're out of your mind. Let me alone!'

Now she could make out two figures in the middle distance. Earl, his paunchy torso spattered and streaked with mud, was on his knees in amongst the soapweed and the scrub. Gyer stood over him, his hands on Earl's head, pressing it down towards the earth.

'Admit your crime, sinner!'

'Damn you, *no*!'

'You came to destroy my crusade. Admit it! Admit it!'

'Go to Hell!'

'Confess your complicity, or so help me I'll break every bone in your body!'

Earl fought to be free of Gyer, but the evangelist was easily the stronger of the two men.

'Pray!' he said, pressing Earl's face into the mud. 'Pray!'

'Go fuck yourself,' Earl shouted back.

Gyer dragged Earl's head up by the hair, his other hand raised to deliver a blow to the upturned face. But before he could strike, Laura-May entered the fray, taking three or four steps through the dirt towards them, the .38 held in her quaking hands.

'Get away from him,' she demanded.

Sadie calmly noted that the woman's aim was not all it could be. Even in clear weather she was probably no sharp-shooter: but here, under stress, in such a downpour, who but the most experienced marksman could guarantee the outcome? Gyer turned and looked at Laura-May. He showed not a flicker of apprehension. He's made the same calculation I've just made, Sadie thought; he knows damn well the odds are against him getting harmed.

'The whore!' Gyer announced, turning his eyes heavenward. 'Do you see her Lord? See her shame, her depravity? Mark her! She is one of the court of Babylon!'

Laura-May didn't quite comprehend the details, but the general thrust of Gyer's outburst was perfectly clear. 'I'm no whore!' she yelled back, the .38 almost leaping in her hand as if eager to be fired. 'Don't you *dare* call me a whore!'

'Please, Laura-May . . .' Earl said, wrestling with Gyer to get a look at the woman, '. . . get out of here. He's lost his mind.'

She ignored the imperative.

'If you don't let go of him . . .' she said, pointing the gun at the man in black.

'Yes?' Gyer taunted her, 'what will you do, *whore?*'

'I'll shoot! *I will!* I'll shoot.'

Over on the other side of the office building, Virginia spotted one of the pill bottles Gyer had thrown out into the mud. She stooped to pick it up, and then thought better of the idea. She didn't need pills any more, did she? She'd spoken to a dead man; her very touch had made Buck Durning visible to her. What a skill that was! Her visions were real, and always had been; more true than all the second-hand Revelations her pitiful husband could spout. What could pills do but befuddle this new-found talent? Let them lie.

144

A number of guests had now donned jackets and emerged from their rooms to see what the commotion was all about.

'Has there been an accident?' a woman called to Virginia. As the words left her lips, a shot sounded.

'John,' Virginia said.

Before the echoes of the shot had died she was making her way towards their source. She already pictured what she would find there: her husband laid flat on the ground; the triumphant assassin taking to his muddied heels. She picked up her pace, a prayer coming as she ran. She prayed not that the scenario she had imagined was wrong; but rather that God would forgive her for willing it to be true.

The scene she found on the other side of the building confounded all her expectations. The evangelist was not dead. He was standing, untouched. It was Earl who lay flat on the miry ground beside him. Close by stood the woman who'd come with the iced water, hours earlier; she had a gun in her hand. It still smoked. Even as Virginia's eyes settled on Laura-May a figure stepped through the rain and struck the weapon from the woman's hand. It fell to the ground. Virginia followed the descent. Laura-May looked startled; she clearly didn't understand how she'd come to drop the gun. Virginia knew, however. She could see the phantom, albeit fleetingly, and she guessed its identity. This was surely Sadie Durning, she whose defiance had christened this establishment the Slaughterhouse of Love.

Laura-May's eyes found Earl; she let out a cry of horror, and ran towards him.

'Don't be dead, Earl. I beg you, don't be dead!'

Earl looked up from the mud bath he'd taken and shook his head.

'Missed me by a mile,' he said.

At his side, Gyer had fallen to his knees, hands clasped together, face up to the driving rain.

'Oh Lord, I thank you for preserving this your instrument, in his hour of need . . .'

Virginia shut out the idiot drivel. This was the man who had convinced her so deeply of her own deluded state that she'd given herself to Buck Durning. Well, *no more*. She'd been terrorized enough. She'd seen Sadie act upon the real world; she'd felt Buck do the same. The time was now ripe to reverse the procedure. She walked steadily across to where the .38 lay in the grass, and picked it up.

As she did so, she sensed the presence of Sadie Durning close by. A voice, so soft she barely heard it, said: 'Is this wise?' in her ear. Virginia didn't know the answer to that question. What *was* wisdom anyhow? Not the stale rhetoric of dead prophets, certainly. Maybe wisdom was Laura-May and Earl, embracing in the mud, careless of the prayers Gyer was spouting, or of the stares of the guests who'd come running out to see who'd died. Or perhaps wisdom was finding the canker in your life, and rooting it out once and for all. Gun in hand, she headed back towards Room Seven, aware that the benign presence of Sadie Durning walked at her side.

'Not Buck . . .?' Sadie whispered, '. . . surely not.'

'He attacked me,' Virginia said.

'You poor lamb.'

'I'm no lamb,' Virginia replied. 'Not any more.'

Realizing that the woman was perfectly in charge of her destiny, Sadie hung back, fearful that her presence would alert Buck. She watched as Virginia crossed the lot, past the cottonwood tree, and stepped into the room where her tormentor had said he would be waiting. The lights still burned, bright after the blue darkness outside. There was no sign of Durning. Virginia crossed to the interconnecting door. Room Eight was deserted too. Then, the familiar voice:

'You came back,' Buck said.

She wheeled round, hiding the gun from him. He had emerged from the bathroom and was standing between her and the door.

'I knew you'd come back,' he said to her. 'They always do.'

'I want you to show yourself –' Virginia said.

'I'm naked as a babe as it is,' said Buck, 'what do you want me to do: skin myself? Might be fun, at that.'

'Show yourself to John, my husband. Make him see his error.'

'Oh, poor John. I don't think he wants to see me, do you?'

'He thinks I'm insane.'

'Insanity can be very useful,' Buck smirked, 'they almost saved Sadie from Old Sparky on a plea of insanity. But she was too honest for her own good. She just kept telling them, over and over: "I wanted him dead. So I shot him." She never had much sense. But you . . . now, I think *you* know what's best for you.'

The shadowy form shifted. Virginia couldn't quite make out what Durning was doing with himself but it was unequivocally obscene.

'Come and get it, Virginia,' he said, 'grub's up.'

She took the .38 from behind her back and levelled it at him.

'Not this time,' she said.

'You can't do me any harm with that,' he replied, 'I'm already dead, remember?'

'*You hurt me*. Why shouldn't I be able to hurt you back?'

Buck shook his ethereal head, letting out a low laugh. As he was so engaged the wail of police sirens rose from down the highway.

147

'Well, what do you know?' Buck said. 'Such a fuss and commotion. We'd better get down to some jazzing, honey, before we get interrupted.'

'I warn you, this is Sadie's gun –'

'You wouldn't hurt me,' Buck murmured, 'I know you women. You say one thing and you mean the opposite.'

He stepped towards her, laughing.

'Don't,' she warned.

He took another step, and she pulled the trigger. In the instant before she heard the sound, and felt the gun leap in her hand, she saw John appear in the doorway. Had he been there all along, or was he coming in out of the rain, prayers done, to read Revelations to his erring wife? She would never know. The bullet sliced through Buck, dividing the smoky body as it went, and sped with perfect accuracy towards the evangelist. He didn't see it coming. It struck him in the throat, and blood came quickly, splashing down his shirt. Buck's form dissolved like so much dust, and he was gone. Suddenly there was nothing in Room Seven but Virginia, her dying husband and the sound of the rain.

John Gyer frowned at Virginia, then reached out for the door frame to support his considerable bulk. He failed to secure it, and fell backwards out of the door like a toppled statue, his face washed by the rain. The blood did not stop coming however. It poured out in gleeful spurts; and it was still pumping when Alvin Baker and his Deputy arrived outside the room, guns at the ready.

Now her husband would never know, she thought: that was the pity of it. He could never now be made to concede his stupidity, and recant his arrogance. Not this side of the grave, anyhow. He was *safe*, damn him, and she was left with a smoking gun in her hand and God alone knew what price to pay.

'Put down the gun and come out of there!' The voice from the lot sounded harsh and uncompromising.

Virginia didn't answer.

'You hear me, in there? This is Sheriff Baker. The place is surrounded, so come on out, or you're dead.'

Virginia sat on the bed and weighed up the alternatives. They wouldn't execute her for what she'd done, the way they had Sadie. But she'd be in prison for a long time, and she was tired of regimes. If she wasn't mad now, incarceration would push her to the brink and over. Better to finish here, she thought. She put the warm .38 under her chin, tilting it to make sure the shot would take off the top of her skull.

'Is that wise?' Sadie inquired, as Virginia's finger tightened.

'They'll lock me away,' she replied, 'I couldn't face that.'

'True,' said Sadie. 'They'll put you behind bars for a while. But it won't be for long.'

'You must be joking. I just shot my husband in cold blood.'

'You didn't mean to,' Sadie said brightly, 'you were aiming at Buck.'

'Was I?' Virginia said. 'I wonder.'

'You can plead insanity, the way I should have done. Just make up the most outrageous story you can, and stick to it.' Virginia shook her head; she'd never been much of a liar. 'And when you're set free,' Sadie went on, 'you'll be notorious. That's worth living for, isn't it?'

Virginia hadn't thought of that. The ghost of a smile illuminated her face. From outside, Sheriff Baker repeated his demand that she throw her weapon through the door and come out with her hands high.

'You've got ten seconds, lady,' he said, 'and I mean *ten*.'

'I can't face the humiliation,' Virginia murmured. 'I *can't*.'

Sadie shrugged. 'Pity,' she said. 'The rain's clearing. There's a moon.'

'A moon? Really?'

Baker had started counting.

'You have to make up your mind,' Sadie said. 'They'll shoot you given half the chance. And gladly.'

Baker had reached eight. Virginia stood up.

'*Stop*,' she called through the door.

Baker stopped counting. Virginia threw out the gun. It landed in the mud.

'Good,' said Sadie, 'I'm so pleased.'

'I can't go alone,' Virginia replied.

'No need.'

A sizeable audience had gathered in the lot; Earl and Laura-May of course; Milton Cade, Dwayne and his girl, Sheriff Baker and his Deputy, an assortment of motel guests. They stood in respectful silence, staring at Virginia Gyer with mingled expressions of bewilderment and awe.

'Put your hands up where I can see them!' Baker said.

Virginia did as she was instructed.

'Look,' said Sadie, pointing.

The moon was up, wide and white.

'Why'd you kill him?' Dwayne's girl asked.

'The Devil made me do it,' Virginia replied, gazing up at the moon and putting on the craziest smile she could muster.

DOWN, SATAN!

CIRCUMSTANCES HAD MADE Gregorius rich beyond all calculation. He owned fleets and palaces; stallions; cities. Indeed he owned so much that to those who were finally charged with enumerating his possessions – when the events of this story reached their monstrous conclusion – it sometimes seemed it might be quicker to list the items Gregorius did *not* own.

Rich he was; but far from happy. He had been raised a Catholic, and in his early years – before his dizzying rise to fortune – he'd found succour in his faith. But he'd neglected it, and it was only at the age of fifty-five, with the world at his feet, that he woke one night and found himself Godless.

It was a bitter blow, but he immediately took steps to make good his loss. He went to Rome, and spoke with the Supreme Pontiff; he prayed night and day; he founded seminaries and leper-colonies. God, however, declined to show so much as His toe-nail. Gregorius, it seemed, was forsaken.

Almost despairing, he took it into his head that he could only win his way back into the arms of his Maker if he put his soul into the direst jeopardy. The notion had some merit. Suppose, he thought, I could contrive a meeting with Satan, the Arch-Fiend; seeing me *in extremis* would God not be obliged to step in and deliver me back into the fold?

It was a fine plot, but how was he to realise it? The Devil did not just come at a call, even for a tycoon such as Gregorius, and his researches soon proved that all the traditional methods of summoning the Lord of Vermin – the defiling of the Blessed Sacrament, the sacrificing of babes – were no more effective than his good works had been at provoking Yahweh. It was only after a year of deliberation that he finally fell upon his master-plan. He would arrange to have built a Hell on Earth – a modern inferno so monstrous that the Tempter would be tempted, and come to roost there like a cuckoo in a usurped nest.

He searched high and low for an architect, and found, languishing in a mad-house outside Florence, a man called Leopardo, whose plans for Mussolini's palaces had a lunatic grandeur that suited Gregorius' project perfectly. Leopardo was taken from his cell – a foetid, wretched old man – and given his dreams again. His genius for the prodigious had not deserted him.

In order to fuel his invention the great libraries of the world were scoured for descriptions of Hells both secular and metaphysical; museum vaults were ransacked for forbidden images of martyrdom. No stone was left unturned if it was suspected something perverse was concealed beneath.

The finished designs owed something to de Sade and to Dante, and something more to Freud and Kraft-Ebbing, but there was also much there that no mind had conceived of before, or at least ever dared set to paper.

A site in North Africa was chosen, and work on Gregorius' New Hell began. Everything about the project broke the records. Its foundations were vaster, its walls thicker, its plumbing more elaborate than any edifice hitherto attempted. Gregorius watched its slow construction with an enthusiasm he had not tasted since his first years as an empire-builder. Needless to say, he was widely thought to have lost his mind. Friends he had known for years refused to associate with him; several of his companies collapsed when investors took fright at reports of his insanity. He didn't care. His plan could not fail. The Devil would be bound to come, if only out of curiosity to see this Leviathan built in his name, and when he did Gregorius would be waiting.

The work took four years, and the better part of Gregorius' fortune. The finished building was the size of half a dozen cathedrals, and boasted every facility the Angel of the Pit could desire. Fires burned behind its walls, so that to walk in many of its corridors was almost unendurable agony. The rooms off those corridors were fitted with every imaginable device of persecution – the needle, the rack, the dark – that the genius of Satan's torturers be given fair employ. There were ovens large enough to cremate families; pools deep enough to drown generations. The New Hell was an atrocity waiting to happen; a celebration of inhumanity that only lacked its first cause.

The builders withdrew, and thankfully. It was rumoured amongst them that Satan had long been watching over the construction of his pleasure-dome. Some even claimed to have glimpsed him on the deeper levels, where the chill was so profound it froze the piss in your bladder. There was some evidence to support the belief in supernatural presences converging on the building as it neared completion, not least the cruel death of Leopardo, who had either thrown himself –

or, the superstitious argued – been pitched, *through* his sixth-storey hotel window. He was buried with due extravagance.

So now, alone in Hell, Gregorius waited.

He did not have to wait long. He had been there a day, no more, when he heard noises from the lower depths. Anticipation brimming, he went in search of their source, but found only the roiling of excrement baths, and the rattling of ovens. He returned to his suite of chambers on the ninth level, and waited. The noises came again; again he went in search of their source; again he came away disappointed.

The disturbances did not abate, however. In the days that followed scarcely ten minutes would pass without his hearing some sound of occupancy. The Prince of Darkness was here, Gregorius could have no doubt of it, but he was keeping to the shadows. Gregorius was content to play along. It was the Devil's party, after all. His to play whatever game he chose.

But, during the long and often lonely months that followed, Gregorius wearied of this hide-and-seek, and began to demand that Satan show himself. His voice rang unanswered down the deserted corridors however, until his throat was bruised with shouting. Thereafter he went about his searches stealthily, hoping to catch his tenant unawares. But the Apostate Angel always flitted away before Gregorius could step within sight of him.

They would play a wasting-game, it seemed, he and Satan, chasing each other's tails through ice and fire and ice again. Gregorius told himself to be patient. The Devil had come, hadn't he? Wasn't that his finger-dab on the door-handle? His turd on the stairs? Sooner or later the Fiend would show his face, and Gregorius would spit on it.

154

The world outside went on its way, and Gregorius was consigned to the company of other recluses who had been ruined by wealth. His Folly, as it was known, was not entirely without visitors, however. There were a few who had loved him too much to forget him – a few, also, who had profited by him, and hoped to turn his madness to their further profit – who dared the gates of the New Hell. These visitors made the journey without announcing their intentions, fearing the disapproval of their friends. The investigations into their subsequent disappearance never reached as far as North Africa.

And in his Folly, Gregorius still chased the Serpent, and the Serpent still eluded him, leaving only more and more terrible signs of his occupancy as the months went by.

It was the wife of one of the missing visitors who finally discovered the truth, and alerted the authorities. Gregorius' Folly was put under surveillance, and finally – some three years after its completion – a quartet of officers braved the threshold.

Without maintenance, the Folly had begun to deteriorate badly. The lights had failed on many of the levels; its walls had cooled,; its pitch-pits solidified. But as the officers advanced through the gloomy vaults in seach of Gregorius, they came upon ample evidence that despite its decrepit condition the New Hell was in good working order. There were bodies in the ovens, their faces wide and black; there were human remains seated and strung up in many of the rooms, gouged and pricked and slit to death.

Their terror grew with every door they pressed open, every new abomination their fevered eyes fell upon.

Two of the four who crossed the threshold never reached the chamber at its centre. Terror overtook them on their way, and they fled, only to be waylaid in some choked passageway and added to the hundreds who had perished in the Folly since Satan had taken residence.

Of the pair who finally unearthed the perpetrator, only one had courage enough to tell his story, though the scenes he faced there in the Folly's heart were almost too terrible to bear relating.

There was no sign of Satan, of course. There was only Gregorius. The master-builder, finding no-one to inhabit the house he had sweated over, had occupied it himself. He had with him a few disciples whom he'd mustered over the years. They, like him, seemed unremarkable creatures. But there was not a torture-device in the building they had not made thorough and merciless use of.

Gregorius did not resist his arrest; indeed he seemed pleased to have a platform from which to boast of his butcheries. Then, and later at his trial, he spoke freely of his ambition and his appetite; and of how much *more* blood he would spill if they would only set him free to do so. Enough to drown all belief and its delusions, he swore. And still he would not be satisfied. For God was rotting in Paradise, and Satan in the Abyss, and who was to stop him?

He was much reviled during the trial, and later in the asylum where, under some suspicious circumstances, he died barely two months later. The Vatican expunged all report of him from its records; the seminaries founded in his unholy name were dissolved.

But there were those, even amongst the Cardinals, who could not put his unrepentant malice out of their heads, and – in the privacy of their doubt – wondered if he had not succeeded in his strategy. If, in giving up all hope of angels – fallen or otherwise – he had not become one himself.

Or all that Earth could bear of such phenomena.

THE AGE OF DESIRE

T HE BURNING MAN propelled himself down the steps of the Hume Laboratories as the police car – summoned, he presumed, by the alarm either Welles or Dance had set off upstairs – appeared at the gate and swung up the driveway. As he ran from the door the car screeched up to the steps and discharged its human cargo. He waited in the shadows, too exhausted by terror to run any further, certain that they would see him. But they disappeared through the swing doors without so much as a glance towards his torment. Am I on fire at all? he wondered. Was this horrifying spectacle – his flesh baptized with a polished flame that seared but failed to consume – simply an hallucination, for his eyes and his eyes only? If so, perhaps all that he had suffered up in the laboratory had also been delirium. Perhaps he had not truly committed the crimes he had fled from, the heat in his flesh licking him into ecstasies.

He looked down his body. His exposed skin still crawled with livid dots of fire, but one by one they were being extinguished. He was going out, he realized, like a neglected bonfire. The sensations that had suffused him – so intense and so demanding that they had been as like pain as pleasure – were finally deserting his nerve-endings, leaving a numbness for which he was grateful. His body, now appearing from beneath the veil of fire, was in a sorry condition. His skin was a panic-map of scratches, his clothes torn to shreds, his hands sticky with coagulating blood; blood, he knew, that was not his own. There was no avoiding the bitter truth. He *had* done all he had imagined doing. Even now the officers would be staring down at his atrocious handiwork.

He crept away from his niche beside the door and down the driveway, keeping a lookout for the return of the two policemen; neither reappeared. The street beyond the gate was deserted. He started to run. He had managed only a few paces when the alarm in the building behind him was abruptly cut off. For several seconds his ears rang in sympathy with the silenced bell. Then, eerily, he began to hear the sound of heat – the surreptitious murmuring of embers – distant enough that he didn't panic, yet close as his heartbeat.

He limped on, to put as much distance as he could between him and his felonies before they were discovered; but however fast he ran, the heat went with him, safe in some backwater of his gut, threatening with every desperate step he took to ignite him afresh.

It took Dooley several seconds to identify the cacophony he was hearing from the upper floor now that McBride had hushed the alarm bell. It was the high-pitched chattering of monkeys, and it came from one of the many rooms down the corridor to his right.

'Virgil,' he called down the stairwell. 'Get up here.'

Not waiting for his partner to join him, Dooley headed off towards the source of the din. Half-way along the corridor the smell of static and new carpeting gave way to a more pungent combination: urine, disinfectant and rotting fruit. Dooley slowed his advance: he didn't like the smell, any more than he liked the hysteria in the babble of monkey-voices. But McBride was slow in answering his call, and after a short hesitation, Dooley's curiosity got the better of his disquiet. Hand on truncheon, he approached the open door and stepped in. His appearance sparked off another wave of frenzy from the animals, a dozen or so rhesus monkeys. They threw themselves around in their cages, somersaulting, screeching and berating the wiremesh. Their excitement was infectious. Dooley could feel the sweat begin to squeeze from his pores.

'Is there anybody here?' he called out.

The only reply came from the prisoners: more hysteria, more cage-rattling. He stared across the room at them. They stared back, their teeth bared in fear or welcome; Dooley didn't know which, nor did he wish to test their intentions. He kept well clear of the bench on which the cages were lined up as he began a perfunctory search of the laboratory.

'I wondered what the hell the smell was,' McBride said, appearing at the door.

'Just animals,' Dooley replied.

'Don't they ever wash? Filthy buggers.'

'Anything downstairs?'

'Nope,' McBride said, crossing to the cages. The monkeys met his advance with more gymnastics. 'Just the alarm.'

'Nothing up here either,' Dooley said. He was about to add, '*Don't do that*,' to prevent his partner putting his finger to the mesh, but before the words were out one of the animals seized the proffered digit and bit it. McBride wrested his finger free and threw a blow back against the mesh in retaliation. Squealing its anger, the occupant flung its scrawny body about in a lunatic fandango that threatened to pitch cage and monkey alike on to the floor.

'You'll need a tetanus shot for that,' Dooley commented.

'Shit!' said McBride, 'what's wrong with the little bastard anyhow?'

'Maybe they don't like strangers.'

'They're out of their tiny minds.' McBride sucked ruminatively on his finger, then spat. 'I mean, look at them.'

Dooley didn't answer.

'I said, *look* . . .' McBride repeated.

Very quietly, Dooley said: 'Over here.'

'What is it?'

'Just come over here.'

McBride drew his gaze from the row of cages and across the cluttered work-surfaces to where Dooley was staring at the ground, the look on his face one of fascinated revulsion. McBride neglected his finger-sucking and threaded his way amongst the benches and stools to where his partner stood.

'Under there,' Dooley murmured.

On the scuffed floor at Dooley's feet was a woman's beige shoe; beneath the bench was the shoe's owner. To judge by her cramped position she had either been secreted there by the miscreant or had dragged herself out of sight and died in hiding.

'Is she dead?' McBride asked.

'Look at her, for Christ's sake,' Dooley replied, 'she's been torn open.'

'We've got to check for vital signs,' McBride reminded him. Dooley made no move to comply, so McBride squatted down in front of the victim and checked for

160

a pulse at her ravaged neck. There was none. Her skin was still warm beneath his fingers however. A gloss of saliva on her cheek had not yet dried.

Dooley, calling his report through, looked down at the deceased. The worst of her wounds, on the upper torso, were masked by McBride's crouching body. All he could see was a fall of auburn hair and her legs, one foot shoeless, protruding from her hiding place. They were beautiful legs, he thought; he might have whistled after such legs, once upon a time.

'She's a Doctor or a technician,' McBride said, 'she's wearing a lab coat.' Or she had been. In fact the coat had been ripped open, as had the layers of clothing beneath, and then, as if to complete the exhibition, the skin and muscle beneath that. McBride peered into her chest; the sternum had been snapped and the heart teased from its seat, as if her killer had wanted to take it as a keepsake and been interrupted in the act. He perused her without squeamishness; he had always prided himself on his strong stomach.

'Are you satisfied she's dead?'

'Never saw deader.'

'Carnegie's coming down,' Dooley said, crossing to one of the sinks. Careless of fingerprints, he turned on the tap and splashed a handful of cold water on to his face. When he looked up from his ablutions McBride had left off his tête-à-tête with the corpse and was walking down the laboratory towards a bank of machinery.

'What do they do here, for Christ's sake?' he remarked. 'Look at all this stuff.'

'Some kind of research faculty,' Dooley said.

'What do they research?'

'How the hell do I know?' Dooley snapped. The ceaseless chatterings of the monkeys and the proximity

161

of the dead woman, made him want to desert the place. 'Let's leave it be, huh?'

McBride ignored Dooley's request; equipment fascinated him. He stared entranced at the encephalograph and electrocardiograph; at the print-out units still disgorging yards of blank paper on to the floor; at the video display monitors and the consoles. The scene brought the *Marie Celeste* to his mind. This deserted ship of science – still humming some tuneless song to itself as it sailed on, though there was neither Captain nor crew left behind to attend upon it.

Beyond the wall of equipment was a window, no more than a yard square. McBride had assumed it led on to the exterior of the building, but now that he looked more closely he realized it did not. A test-chamber lay beyond the banked units.

'Dooley . . .?' he said, glancing round. The man had gone, however, down to meet Carnegie presumably. Content to be left to his exploration, McBride returned his attention to the window. There was no light on inside. Curious, he walked around the back of the banked equipment, until he found the chamber door. It was ajar. Without hesitation, he stepped through.

Most of the light through the window was blocked by the instruments on the other side; the interior was dark. It took McBride's eyes a few seconds to get a true impression of the chaos the chamber contained: the overturned table; the chair of which somebody had made matchwood; the tangle of cables and demolished equipment – cameras, perhaps, to monitor proceedings in the chamber? – clusters of lights which had been similarly smashed. No professional vandal could have made a more thorough job of breaking up the chamber than had been made.

There was a smell in the air which McBride recognized but, irritatingly, couldn't place. He stood still, tantalized by the scent. The sound of sirens rose from down the corridor outside; Carnegie would be here in moments. Suddenly, the smell's association came to him. It was the same scent that twitched in his nostrils when, after making love to Jessica and – as was his ritual – washing himself, he returned from the bathroom to the bedroom. It was the smell of sex. He smiled.

His face was still registering pleasure when a heavy object sliced through the air and met his nose. He felt the cartilage give, and a rush of blood come. He took two or three giddy steps backwards, thereby avoiding the subsequent slice, but lost his footing in the disarray. He fell awkwardly in a litter of glass shards, and looked up to see his assailant, wielding a metal bar, moving towards him. The man's face resembled one of the monkeys: the same yellowed teeth, the same rabid eyes. '*No!*' the man shouted, as he brought his makeshift club down on McBride, who managed to ward off the blow with his arm, snatching at the weapon in so doing. The attack had taken him unawares but now, with the pain in his mashed nose to add fury to his response, he was more than the equal of the aggressor. He plucked the club from the man, sweets from a babe, and leapt, roaring, to his feet. Any precepts he might once have been taught about arrest techniques had fled from his mind. He lay a hail of blows on the man's head and shoulders, forcing him backwards across the chamber. The man cowered beneath the assault, and eventually slumped, whimpering, against the wall. Only now, with his antagonist abused to the verge of unconsciousness, did McBride's furore falter. He stood in the middle of the chamber, gasping for breath, and watched the beaten man slip down the wall. He had made a profound error. The assailant, he now realized, was dressed in a white laboratory coat; he was, as Dooley was irritatingly fond of saying, on the side of the angels.

163

'Damn,' said McBride, 'shit, hell and damn.'

The man's eyes flickered open, and he gazed up at McBride. His grasp on consciousness was evidently tenuous, but a look of recognition crossed his wide-browed, sombre face. Or rather, recognition's absence.

'You're not him,' he murmured.

'Who?' said McBride, realizing he might yet salvage his reputation from this fiasco if he could squeeze a clue from the witness. 'Who did you think I was?'

The man opened his mouth, but no words emerged. Eager to hear the testimony, McBride crouched beside him and said: 'Who did you think you were attacking?'

Again the mouth opened; again no audible words emerged. McBride pressed his suit. 'It's important,' he said, 'just tell me who was here.'

The man strove to voice his reply. McBride pressed his ear to the trembling mouth.

'In a pig's eye,' the man said, then passed out, leaving McBride to curse his father, who'd bequeathed him a temper he was afraid he would probably live to regret. But then, what was living for?

Inspector Carnegie was used to boredom. For every rare moment of genuine discovery his professional life had furnished him with, he had endured hour upon hour of waiting. For bodies to be photographed and examined, for lawyers to be bargained with and suspects intimidated. He had long ago given up attempting to fight this tide of *ennui* and, after his fashion, had learned the art of going with the flow. The processes of investigation could not be hurried; the wise man, he had come to appreciate, let the pathologists, the lawyers and all their tribes have their tardy way. All that mattered, in the fullness of time, was that the finger be pointed and that the guilty quake.

Now, with the clock on the laboratory wall reading twelve fifty-three a.m., and even the monkeys hushed in their cages, he sat at one of the benches and waited for Hendrix to finish his calculations. The surgeon consulted the thermometer, then stripped off his gloves like a second skin and threw them down on to the sheet on which the deceased lay. 'It's always difficult,' the Doctor said, 'fixing time of death. She's lost less than three degrees. I'd say she's been dead under two hours.'

'The officers arrived at a quarter to twelve,' Carnegie said, 'so she died maybe half an hour before that?'

'Something of that order.'

'Was she put in there?' he asked, indicating the place beneath the bench.

'Oh certainly. There's no way she hid herself away. Not with those injuries. They're quite something, aren't they?'

Carnegie stared at Hendrix. The man had presumably seen hundreds of corpses, in every conceivable condition, but the enthusiasm in his pinched features was unqualified. Carnegie found that mystery more fascinating in its way than that of the dead woman and her slaughterer. How could anyone possibly enjoy taking the rectal temperature of a corpse? It confounded him. But the pleasure was there, gleaming in the man's eyes.

'Motive?' Carnegie asked.

'Pretty explicit, isn't it? Rape. There's been very thorough molestation; contusions around the vagina; copious semen deposits. Plenty to work with.'

'And the wounds on her torso?'

'Ragged. Tears more than cuts.'

'Weapon?'

'Don't know.' Hendrix made an inverted U of his mouth. 'I mean, the flesh has been *mauled*. If it weren't

165

for the rape evidence I'd be tempted to suggest an animal.'

'Dog, you mean?'

'I was thinking more of a tiger,' Hendrix said.

Carnegie frowned. 'Tiger?'

'Joke,' Hendrix replied, 'I was making a joke, Carnegie. My Christ, do you have *any* sense of irony?'

'This isn't funny,' Carnegie said.

'I'm not laughing,' Hendrix replied, with a sour look.

'The man McBride found in the test-chamber?'

'What about him?'

'Suspect?'

'Not in a thousand years. We're looking for a *maniac*, Carnegie. Big; strong. Wild.'

'And the wounding? Before or after?'

Hendrix scowled. 'I don't know. Post-mortem will give us more. But for what it's worth, I think our man was in a frenzy. I'd say the wounding and the rape were probably simultaneous.'

Carnegie's normally phlegmatic features registered something close to shock. 'Simultaneous?'

Hendrix shrugged. 'Lust's a funny thing,' he said.

'Hilarious,' came the appalled reply.

As was his wont, Carnegie had his driver deposit him half a mile from his doorstep to allow him a head-clearing walk before home, hot chocolate and slumber. The ritual was observed religiously, even when the Inspector was dog-tired. He used to stroll to wind down before stepping over the threshold; long experience had taught him that taking his professional concerns into the house assisted neither the investigation nor his domestic life. He had learned the lesson too late to keep his wife from leaving him and his children from estrangement, but he applied the principle still.

166

Tonight, he walked slowly, to allow the distressing scenes the evening had brought to recede somewhat. The route took him past a small cinema which, he had read in the local press, was soon to be demolished. He was not surprised. Though he was no cineaste the fare the flea-pit provided had degenerated in recent years. The week's offering was a case in point: a double-bill of horror movies. Lurid and derivative stuff to judge by the posters, with their crude graphics and their unashamed hyperbole. '*You May Never Sleep Again!*' one of the hook-lines read; and beneath it a woman – very much awake – cowered in the shadow of a two-headed man. What trivial images the populists conjured to stir some fear in their audiences. The walking dead; nature grown vast, and rampant in a miniature world; blood-eaters, omens, fire-walkers, thunderstorms and all the other foolishness the public cowered before. It was all so laughably trite: amongst that catalogue of penny dreadfuls there wasn't one that equalled the banality of human appetite, which horror (or the consequences of same) he saw every week of his working life. Thinking of it, his mind thumbed through a dozen snapshots: the dead by torchlight, face down and thrashed to oblivion; and the living too, meeting his mind's eye with hunger in theirs: for sex, for narcotics, for others' pain. Why didn't they put *that* on the posters?

As he reached his home a child squealed in the shadows beside his garage; the cry stopped him in his tracks. It came again, and this time he recognized it for what it was. No child at all, but a cat, or cats, exchanging love-calls in the darkened passageway. He went to the place to shoo them off. Their venereal secretions made the passage stink. He didn't need to yell; his footfall was sufficient to scare them away. They darted in all directions, not two, but half a dozen of them: a veritable orgy had been underway apparently. He had arrived on

167

the spot too late however; the stench of their seductions was overpowering.

Carnegie looked blankly at the elaborate set-up of monitors and video-recorders that dominated his office.

'What in Christ's name is this about?' he wanted to know.

'The video tapes,' said Boyle, his number two, 'from the laboratory. I think you ought to have a look at them. Sir.'

Though they had worked in tandem for seven months, Boyle was not one of Carnegie's favourite officers; you could practically smell the ambition off his smooth hide. In someone half his age again such greed would have been objectionable; in a man of thirty it verged on the obscene. This present display – the mustering of equipment ready to confront Carnegie when he walked in at eight in the morning – was just Boyle's style: flashy and redundant.

'Why so many screens?' Carnegie asked acidly. 'Do I get it in stereo too?'

'They had three cameras running simultaneously, sir. Covering the experiment from several angles.'

'*What* experiment?'

Boyle gestured for his superior to sit down. Obsequious to a fault, aren't you, thought Carnegie; much good it'll do you.

'Right,' Boyle instructed the technician at the recorders, 'roll the tapes.'

Carnegie sipped at the cup of hot chocolate he had brought in with him. The beverage was a weakness of his, verging on addiction. On the days when the machine supplying it broke down he was an unhappy man indeed. He looked at the three screens. Suddenly, a title.

'*Project Blind Boy*', the words read, '*Restricted*.'

'*Blind Boy*?' said Carnegie. 'What, or *who*, is that?'

'It's obviously a code word of some kind,' Boyle said.

'*Blind Boy. Blind Boy.*' Carnegie repeated the phrase as if to beat it into submission, but before he could solve the problem the images on the three monitors diverged. They pictured the same subject – a bespectacled male in his late twenties sitting in a chair – but each showed the scene from a different angle. One took in the subject full length, and in profile; the second was a three-quarter medium shot, angled from above; the third a straight forward close up of the subject's head and shoulders, shot through the glass of the test-chamber, and from the front. The three images were in black and white, and none were completely centred or focused. Indeed, as the tapes began to run, somebody was still adjusting such technicalities. A backwash of informal chatter ran between the subject and the woman – recognizable even in brief glimpses as the deceased – who was applying electrodes to his forehead. Much of the talk between them was difficult to catch; the acoustics in the chamber frustrated microphone and listener alike.

'The woman's Doctor Dance,' Boyle offered. 'The victim.'

'Yes,' said Carnegie, watching the screens intently, 'I recognize her. How long does this preparation go on for?'

'Quite a while. Most of it's unedifying.'

'Well, get to the edifying stuff, then.'

'Fast forward,' Boyle said. The technician obliged, and the actors on the three screens became squeaking comedians. 'Wait!' said Boyle. 'Back up a short way.' Again, the technician did as instructed. 'There!' said Boyle. 'Stop there. Now run on at normal speed.' The action settled back to its natural pace. 'This is where it really begins, sir.'

Carnegie had come to the end of his hot chocolate; he put his finger into the soft sludge at the bottom of the cup, delivering the sickly-sweet dregs to his tongue. On the screens Doctor Dance had approached the subject with a syringe, was now swabbing the crook of his elbow, and injecting him. Not for the first time since his visit to the Hume Laboratories did Carnegie wonder precisely what they did at the establishment. Was this kind of procedure *de rigeur* in pharmaceutical research? The implicit secrecy of the experiment – late at night in an otherwise deserted building – suggested not. And there was that imperative on the title-card – '*Restricted*'. What they were watching had clearly never been intended for public viewing.

'Are you comfortable?' a man, off camera, now enquired. The subject nodded. His glasses had been removed, and he looked slightly bemused without them. An unremarkable face, thought Carnegie; the subject – as yet unnamed – was neither Adonis nor Quasimodo. He was receding slightly, and his wispy, dirty blond hair touched his shoulders.

'I'm fine, Doctor Welles,' he replied to the off-camera questioner.

'You don't feel hot at all? Sweaty?'

'Not really,' the guinea-pig replied, slightly apologetically. 'I feel ordinary.'

That you are, Carnegie thought; then to Boyle: 'Have you been through the tapes to the end?'

'No, sir,' Boyle replied. 'I thought you'd want to see them first. I only ran them as far as the injection.'

'Any word from the hospital on Doctor Welles?'

'At the last call he was still comatose.'

Carnegie grunted, and returned his attention to the screens. Following the burst of action with the injection, the tapes now settled into non-activity: the three cameras fixed on their short-sighted subject with beady stares, the torpor occasionally interrupted by an enquiry from Welles as to the subject's condition. It remained the

170

same. After three or four minutes of this eventless study even his occasional blinks began to assume major dramatic significance.

'Don't think much of the plot,' the technician commented. Carnegie laughed; Boyle looked discomforted. Two or three more minutes passed in a similar manner.

'This doesn't look too hopeful,' Carnegie said. 'Run through it at speed, will you?'

The technician was about to obey when Boyle said: '*Wait.*'

Carnegie glanced across at the man, irritated by his intervention, and then back at the screens. Something *was* happening: a subtle transformation had overtaken the insipid features of the subject. He had begun to smile to himself, and was sinking down in his chair as if submerging his gangling body in a warm bath. His eyes, which had so far expressed little but affable indifference, now began to flicker closed, and then, once closed, opened again. When they did so there was a quality in them not previously visible: a hunger that seemed to reach out from the screen and into the calm of the Inspector's office.

Carnegie put down his chocolate cup and approached the screens. As he did so the subject also got up out of his chair and walked towards the glass of the chamber, leaving two of the cameras' ranges. The third still recorded him however, as he pressed his face against the window, and for a moment the two men faced each other through layers of glass and time, seemingly meeting each other's gaze.

The look on the man's face was critical now, the hunger was rapidly outgrowing sane control. Eyes burning, he laid his lips against the chamber window and kissed it, his tongue working against the glass.

'What in Christ's name is going on?' Carnegie said.

A prattle of voices had begun on the soundtrack;

171

Doctor Welles was vainly asking the testee to articulate his feelings, while Dance called off figures from the various monitoring instruments. It was difficult to hear much clearly – the din was further supplemented by an eruption of chatter from the caged monkeys – but it was evident that the readings coming through from the man's body were escalating. His face was flushed; his skin gleamed with a sudden sweat. He resembled a martyr with the tinder at his feet freshly lit; wild with a fatal ecstasy. He stopped french-kissing the window, tearing off the electrodes at his temples and the sensors from his arms and chest. Dance, her voice now registering alarm, called out for him to stop. Then she moved across the camera's view and out again; crossing, Carnegie presumed, to the chamber door.

'Better not,' he said, as if this drama were played out at his behest, and at a whim he could prevent the tragedy. But the woman took no notice. A moment later she appeared in long shot as she stepped into the chamber. The man moved to greet her, throwing over equipment as he did so. She called out to him – his name, perhaps. If so, it was inaudible over the monkeys' hullabaloo. 'Shit,' said Carnegie, as the testee's flailing arms caught first the profile camera, and then the three-quarter medium shot: two of the three monitors went dead. Only the head-on shot, the camera safe outside the chamber, still recorded events, but the tightness of the shot precluded more than an occasional glimpse of a moving body. Instead, the camera's sober eye gazed on, almost ironically, at the saliva smeared glass of the chamber window, blind to the atrocities being committed a few feet out of range.

'What in Christ's name did they give him?' Carnegie said, as, somewhere off-camera, the woman's screams rose over the screeching of the apes.

* * *

172

Jerome woke in the early afternoon, feeling hungry and sore. When he threw the sheet off his body he was appalled at his state: his torso was scored with scratches, and his groin region was re-draw. Wincing, he moved to the edge of the bed and sat there for a while, trying to piece the previous evening back together again. He remembered going to the Laboratories, but very little after that. He had been a paid guinea-pig for several months, giving of his blood, comfort and patience to supplement his meagre earnings as a translator. The arrangement had begun courtesy of a friend who did similar work, but whereas Figley had been part of the Laboratories' mainstream programme, Jerome had been approached, after one week at the place, by Doctors Welles and Dance, who had invited him – subject to a series of psychological tests – to work exclusively for them. It had been made clear from the outset that their project (he had never even been told its purpose) was of a secret nature, and that they would demand his total dedication and discretion. He had needed the funds, and the recompense they offered was marginally better than that paid by the Laboratories, so he had agreed, although the hours they had demanded of him were unsociable. For several weeks now he had been required to attend the Research facility late at night and often working into the small hours of the morning as he endured Welles' interminable questions about his private life, and Dance's glassy stare.

Thinking of her cold look, he felt a tremor in him. Was it because once he had fooled himself that she had looked upon him more fondly than a doctor need? Such self-deception, he chided himself, was pitiful. He was not the stuff of which women dreamt, and each day he walked the streets reinforced that conviction. He could not remember one occasion in his adult life when a woman had looked his way, and kept looking; a time when an appreciative glance of his had been returned. Why this should bother him now, he wasn't certain: his loveless condition, was, he knew, commonplace. And Nature had been kind; knowing, it seemed, that the gift of allurement had passed him by, it had seen fit to minimize his libido. Weeks passed without his conscious thoughts mourning his enforced chastity.

Once in a while, when he heard the pipes roar, he might wonder what Mrs Morrisey, his landlady, looked like in her bath: might imagine the firmness of her soapy breasts, or the dark divide of her rump as she stooped to put talcum powder between her toes. But such torments were, blissfully, infrequent. And when his cup brimmed he would pocket the money he had saved from his sessions at the Laboratories, and buy an hour's companionship from a woman called Angela (he'd never learned her second name) in Greek Street.

It would be several weeks before he did so again, he thought: whatever he had done last night, or, more correctly, had done to him, the bruises alone had nearly crippled him. The only plausible explanation – though he couldn't recall any details – was that he'd been beaten up on the way back from the Laboratories; either that, or he'd stepped into a bar and somebody had picked a fight with him. It had happened before, on occasion. He had one of those faces that awoke the bully in drunkards.

He stood up and hobbled to the small bathroom adjoining his room. His glasses were missing from their normal spot beside the shaving mirror, and his reflection was woefully blurred, but it was apparent that his face was as badly scratched as the rest of his anatomy And more: a clump of hair had been pulled out from above his left ear; clotted blood ran down to his neck Painfully, he bent to the task of cleaning his wounds then bathing them in a stinging solution of antiseptic That done, he returned into his bedsitting-room to seek

174

out his spectacles. But search as he might, he could not locate them. Cursing his idiocy, he rooted amongst his belongings for his old pair, and found them. Their prescription was out of date – his eyes had worsened considerably since he'd worn them – but they at least brought his surroundings into a dreamy kind of focus.

An indisputable melancholy had crept up on him, compounded of his pain and those unwelcome thoughts of Mrs Morrisey. To keep its intimacy at bay he turned on the radio. A sleek voice emerged, purveying the usual palliatives. Jerome had always had contempt for popular music and its apologists, but now, as he mooched around the small room, unwilling to clothe himself with chafing weaves when his scratches still pained him, the songs began to stir something other than scorn in him. It was as though he was hearing the words and music for the first time: as though all his life he had been deaf to their sentiments. Enthralled, he forgot his pain, and listened. The songs told one seamless and obsessive story: of love lost and found, only to be lost again. The lyricists filled the airwaves with metaphor – much of it ludicrous, but no less potent for that. Of paradise, of hearts on fire; of birds, bells, journeys, sunsets; of passion as lunacy, as flight, as unimaginable treasure. The songs did not calm him with their fatuous sentiments; they flayed him, evoking, despite feeble rhyme and trite melody, a world bewitched by desire. He began to tremble. His eyes, strained (or so he reasoned) by the unfamiliar spectacles, began to delude him. It seemed as though he could see traces of light in his skin: sparks flying from the ends of his fingers.

He stared at his hands and arms; the illusion, far from retreating in the face of this scrutiny, increased. Beads of brightness, like the traces of fire in ash, began to climb through his veins, multiplying even as he watched. Curiously, he felt no distress. This burgeoning fire

175

merely reflected the passion in the story the songs were telling him: love, they said, was in the air, round every corner, waiting to be found. He thought again of the widow Morrisey in the flat below him, going about her business, sighing, no doubt, as he had done; awaiting her hero. The more he thought of her the more inflamed he became. She would not reject him, of that the songs convinced him; or if she did he must press his case until (again, as the songs promised) she surrendered to him. Suddenly, at the thought of her surrender, the fire engulfed him. Laughing, he left the radio singing behind him, and made his way downstairs.

It had taken the best part of the morning to assemble a list of testees employed at the Laboratories; Carnegie had sensed a reluctance on the part of the establishment to open their files to the investigation, despite the horror that had been committed on its premises. Finally, just after noon, they had presented him with a hastily assembled Who's Who of subjects, four and a half dozen *in toto*, and their addresses. None, the offices claimed, matched the description of Welles' testee. The Doctors, it was explained, had been clearly using Laboratory facilities to work on private projects. Though this was not encouraged, both had been senior researchers, and allowed leeway on the matter. It was likely, therefore, that the man Carnegie was seeking had never even been on the Laboratories' payroll. Undaunted, Carnegie ordered a selection of photographs taken off the video recording and had them distributed – with the list of names and addresses – to his officers. From then on, it was down to footwork and patience.

Leo Boyle ran his finger down the list of names he had been given. 'Another fourteen,' he said. His driver grunted, and Boyle glanced across at him. 'You were McBride's partner, weren't you?' he said.

'That's right,' Dooley replied. 'He's been suspended.'

'Why?'

Dooley scowled. 'Lacks finesse, does Virgil. Can't get the hang of arrest technique.'

Dooley drew the car to a halt.

'Is this it?' Boyle asked.

'You said number eighty. This is eighty. On the door. Eight. Oh.'

'I've got eyes.'

Boyle got out of the car and made his way up the pathway. The house was sizeable, and had been divided into flats: there were several bells. He pressed for J. Tredgold – the name on his list – and waited. Of the five houses they had so far visited, two had been unoccupied and the residents of the other three had borne no resemblance to the malefactor.

Boyle waited on the step a few seconds and then pressed the bell again; a longer ring this time.

'Nobody in,' Dooley said from the pavement.

'Looks like it.' Even as he spoke Boyle caught sight of a figure flitting across the hallway, its outline distorted by the cobblestone glass in the door. 'Wait a minute,' he said.

'What is it?'

'Somebody's in there and not answering.' He pressed the first bell again, and then the others. Dooley approached up the pathway, flitting away an over-attentive wasp.

'You sure?' he said.

'I saw somebody in there.'

'Press the other bells,' Dooley suggested.

'I already did. There's somebody in there and they don't want to come to the door.' He rapped on the glass. 'Open up,' he announced. 'Police.'

Clever, thought Dooley; why not a loud-hailer, so Heaven knows too? When the door, predictably, remained unanswered, Boyle turned to Dooley. 'Is there a side gate?'

'Yes, sir.'

'Then get round the back, pronto, before he's away.'

'Shouldn't we call –?'

'Do it! I'll keep watch here. If you can get in the back come through and open the front door.'

Dooley moved; leaving Boyle alone at the front door. He rang the series of bells again, and, cupping his hand to his brow, put his face to the glass. There was no sign of movement in the hallway; was it possible that the bird had already flown? He backed down the path and stared up at the windows; they stared back vacuously. Ample time had now passed for Dooley to get round the back of the house; but so far he had neither reappeared nor called. Stymied where he stood, and nervous that his tactics had lost them their quarry, Boyle decided to follow his nose around the back of the house.

The side gate had been left open by Dooley. Boyle advanced up the side passage, glancing through a window into an empty living-room before heading round the back door. It was open. Dooley, however, was not in sight. Boyle pocketed the photograph and the list, and stepped inside, loath to the call Dooley's name for fear it alert any felon to his presence, yet nervous of the silence. Cautious as a cat on broken glass he crept through the flat, but each room was deserted. At the flat door, which let on to the hallway in which he had first seen the figure, he paused. Where had Dooley gone? The man had apparently disappeared from sight.

Then, a groan from beyond the door.

'Dooley?' Boyle ventured. Another groan. He stepped into the hallway. Three more doors presented themselves, all were closed; other flats, presumably, or bedsitting rooms. On the coconut mat at the front door lay Dooley's truncheon, dropped there as if its owner had been in the process of making his escape. Boyle swallowed his fear and walked into the body of the hall. The complaint came again, close by. He looked round and up the stairs. There, on the half-landing, lay Dooley. He was barely conscious. A rough attempt had been made to rip his clothes; large portions of his flabby lower anatomy were exposed.

'What's going on, Dooley?' Boyle asked, moving to the bottom of the stairs. The officer heard his voice and rolled himself over. His bleary eyes, settling on Boyle, opened in terror.

'It's all right,' Boyle reassured him. 'It's only me.'

Too late, Boyle registered that Dooley's gaze wasn't fixed on *him* at all, but on some sight over his shoulder. As he pivoted on his heel to snatch a glance at Dooley's bugaboo a charging figure slammed into him. Winded and cursing, Boyle was thrown off his feet. He scrabbled about on the floor for several seconds before his attacker seized hold of him by jacket and hair and hauled him to his feet. He recognized at once the wild face that was thrust into his – the receding hair-line, the weak mouth, the *hunger* – but there was much too he had not anticipated. For one, the man was naked as a babe, though scarcely so modestly endowed. For another, he was clearly aroused to fever-pitch. If the beady eye at his groin, shining up at Boyle, were not evidence enough, the hands now tearing at his clothes made the assailant's intention perfectly apparent.

'Dooley!' Boyle shrieked as he was thrown across the hallway. 'In Christ's name! Dooley!'

His pleas were silenced as he hit the opposite wall. The wild man was at his back in half a heartbeat, smearing Boyle's face against the wallpaper: birds and flowers, intertwined, filled his eyes. In desperation,

179

Boyle fought back, but the man's passion lent him ungovernable strength. With one insolent hand holding the policeman's head, he tore at Boyle's trousers and underwear, leaving his buttocks exposed.

'God . . .' Boyle begged into the pattern of the wall-paper. 'Please God, somebody help me . . .'; but the prayers were no more fruitful than his struggles. He was pinned against the wall like a butterfly spread on cork, about to be pierced through. He closed his eyes, tears of frustration running down his cheeks. The assailant left off his hold on Boyle's head and pressed his violation home. Boyle refused to cry out. The pain he felt was not the equal of his shame. Better perhaps that Dooley remained comatose; that this humiliation be done and finished with unwitnessed.

'Stop,' he murmured into the wall, not to his attacker but to his body, urging it not to find pleasure in this outrage. But his nerve-endings were treacherous; they caught fire from the assault. Beneath the stabbing agony some unforgivable part of him rose to the occasion.

On the stairs, Dooley hauled himself to his feet. His lumbar region, which had been weak since a car accident the previous Christmas, had given out almost as soon as the wild man had sprung him in the hall. Now, as he descended the stairs, the least motion caused excruciating agonies. Crippled with pain, he stumbled to the bottom of the stairs and looked, amazed, across the hallway. Could this be Boyle – he the supercilious, he the rising man, being pummelled like a street-boy in need of dope money? The sight transfixed Dooley for several seconds before he unhinged his eyes and swung them down to the truncheon on the mat. He moved cautiously, but the wild man was too occupied with the deflowering to notice him.

Jerome was listening to Boyle's heart. It was a loud, seductive beat, and with every thrust into the man it seemed to get louder. He wanted it: the heat of it, the life of it. His hand moved round to Boyle's chest, and dug at the flesh.

'Give me your heart,' he said. It was like a line from one of the songs.

Boyle screamed into the wall as his attacker mauled his chest. He'd seen photographs of the woman at the Laboratories; the open wound of her torso was lightning-clear in his mind's eye. Now the maniac intended the same atrocity. *Give me your heart*. Panicked to the ledge of his sanity he found new stamina, and began to fight afresh, reaching round and clawing at the man's torso: nothing – not even the bloody loss of hair from his scalp – broke the rhythm of his thrusts, however. In extremis, Boyle attempted to insinuate one of his hands between his body and the wall and reach between his legs to unman the bastard. As he did so, Dooley attacked, delivering a hail of truncheon blows upon the man's head. The diversion gave Boyle precious leeway. He pressed hard against the wall; the man, his grip on Boyle's chest slicked with blood, lost his hold. Again, Boyle pushed. This time, he managed to shrug the man off entirely. The bodies disengaged; Boyle turned, bleeding but in no danger, and watched Dooley follow the man across the hallway, beating at his greasy blond head. He made little attempt to protect himself however: his burning eyes (Boyle had never understood the physical accuracy of that image until now) were still on the object of his affections.

'Kill him!' Boyle said quietly, as the man grinned – grinned! – through the blows. 'Break every bone in his body!'

Even if Dooley, hobbled as he was, had been in any fit state to obey the imperative, he had no chance to do so. His berating was interrupted by a voice from down the hallway. A woman had emerged from the flat Boyle

181

had come through. She too had been a victim of this marauder, to judge by her state; but Dooley's entry into the house had clearly distracted her molester before he could do serious damage.

'Arrest him!' she said, pointing at the leering man. 'He tried to rape me!'

Dooley closed in to take possession of the prisoner, but Jerome had other intentions. He put his hand in Dooley's face and pushed him back against the front door. The coconut mat slid from under him: he all but fell. By the time he'd regained his balance Jerome was up and away. Boyle made a wretched attempt to stop him, but the tatters of his trousers were wrapped about his lower legs and Jerome, fleet-footed, was soon half-way up the stairs.

'Call for help,' Boyle ordered Dooley. 'And make it quick.'

Dooley nodded, and opened the front door.

'Is there any way out from upstairs?' Boyle demanded of Mrs Morrisey. She shook her head. 'Then we've got the bastard trapped haven't we?' he said. 'Go on, Dooley!' Dooley hobbled away down the path. 'And you,' he said to the woman, 'fetch something in the way of weaponry. Anything solid.' The woman nodded and returned the way she'd come, leaving Boyle slumped beside the open door. A soft breeze cooled the sweat on his face. At the car outside Dooley was calling up reinforcements.

All too soon, Boyle thought, the cars would be here, and the man upstairs would be hauled away to give his testimony. There would be no opportunity for revenge once he was in custody; the law would take its placid course, and he, the victim, would be only a by-stander. If he was ever to salvage the ruins of his manhood, *now* was the time. If he didn't – if he languished here, his bowels on fire – he would never shrug off the horror he felt at his body's betrayal. He must act now – must beat the grin off his ravisher's face once and for all – or else live in self-disgust until memory failed him.

The choice was no choice at all. Without further debate, he got up from his squatting position, and began up the stairs. As he reached the half-landing he realized he hadn't brought a weapon with him, he knew, however, that if he descended again he'd lose all momentum. Prepared, in that moment, to die if necessary, he headed on up.

There was only one door open on the top landing; through it came the sound of a radio. Downstairs, in the safety of the hall, he heard Dooley come in to tell him that the call had been made, only to break off in mid-announcement. Ignoring the distraction, Boyle stepped into the flat.

There was nobody there. It took Boyle a few moments only to check the kitchen, the tiny bathroom, and the living room: all were deserted. He returned to the bathroom, the window of which was open, and put his head out. The drop to the grass of the garden below was quite manageable. There was an imprint in the ground of the man's body. He had leapt. And gone.

Boyle cursed his tardiness, and hung his head. A trickle of heat ran down the inside of his leg. In the next room, the love-songs played on.

For Jerome, there was no forgetfulness, not this time. The encounter with Mrs Morrisey, which had been interrupted by Dooley, and the episode with Boyle that had followed, had all merely served to fan the fire in him. Now, by the light of those flames, he saw clearly what crimes he had committed. He remembered with horrible clarity the laboratory, the injection, the monkeys, the blood. The acts he recalled, however (and there were many), woke no sense of sinfulness in him. All moral consequence, all shame or remorse, was burned out by the fire that was even now licking his flesh to new enthusiasms.

He took refuge in a quiet cul-de-sac to make himself presentable. The clothes he had managed to snatch before making his escape were motley, but would serve to keep him from attracting unwelcome attention. As he buttoned himself up – his body seeming to strain from its covering as if resentful of being concealed – he tried to control the holocaust that raged between his ears. But the flames wouldn't be dampened. His every fibre seemed alive to the flux and flow of the world around him. The marshalled trees along the road, the wall at his back, the very paving stones beneath his bare feet were catching a spark from him, and burning now with their own fire. He grinned to see the conflagration spread. The world, in its every eager particular, grinned back.

Aroused beyond control, he turned to the wall he had been leaning against. The sun had fallen full upon it, and it was warm: the bricks smelt ambrosial. He laid kisses on their gritty faces, his hands exploring every nook and cranny. Murmuring sweet nothings, he unzipped himself, found an accommodating niche, and filled it. His mind was running with liquid pictures: mingled anatomies, female and male in one undistinguishable congress. Above him, even the clouds had caught fire; enthralled by their burning heads he felt the moment rise in his gristle. Breath was short now. But the ecstasy? Surely that would go on forever.

Without warning a spasm of pain travelled down his spine from cortex to testicles, and back again, convulsing him. His hands lost grip of the brick and he finished his agonizing climax on the air as he fell across the pavement. For several seconds he lay where he had collapsed, while the echoes of the initial spasm bounced back and forth along his spine, diminishing with each return. He could taste blood at the back of his throat; he wasn't certain if he'd bitten his lip or tongue, but he thought not. Above his head the birds circled on, rising lazily on a spiral of warm air. He watched the fire in the clouds gutter out.

He got to his feet and looked down at the coinage of semen he'd spent on the pavement. For a fragile instant he caught again a whiff of the vision he'd just had; imagined a marriage of his seed with the paving stone. What sublime children the world might boast, he thought, if he could only mate with brick or tree; he would gladly suffer the agonies of conception, if such miracles were possible. But the paving stone was unmoved by his seed's entreaties; the vision, like the fire above him, cooled and hid its glories.

He put his bloodied member away, and leaned against the wall, turning the strange events of his recent life over and over. Something fundamental was changing in him, of that he had no doubt; the rapture that had possessed him (and would, no doubt, possess him again) was like nothing he had hitherto experienced. And whatever they had injected into his system it showed no signs of being discharged naturally; far from it. He could feel the heat in him still, as he had leaving the Laboratories; but this time the roar of its presence was louder than ever.

It was a new kind of life he was living, and the thought, though frightening, exulted him. Not once did it occur to his spinning, eroticized brain that this new kind of life would, in time, demand a new kind of death.

Carnegie had been warned by his superiors that results were expected; he was now passing the verbal beating he'd received to those under him. It was a line of humiliation, in which the greater was encouraged to kick the lesser man, and that man, in turn, his lesser.

Carnegie had sometimes wondered what the man at the end of the line took his ire out on; his dog presumably.

'This miscreant is still loose, gentlemen, despite his photograph in many of this morning's newspapers, and an operating method which is, to say the least, insolent. We *will* catch him, of course, but let's get the bastard before we have another murder on our hands –'

The phone rang. Boyle's replacement, Migeon, picked it up, while Carnegie concluded his pep-talk to the assembled officers.

'I want him in the next twenty-four hours, gentlemen. That's the time-scale I've been given, and that's what we've got. Twenty-four hours.'

Migeon interrupted. 'Sir? It's Johannson. He says he's got something for you. It's urgent.'

'Right.' The Inspector claimed the receiver. 'Carnegie.'

The voice at the other end was soft to the point of inaudibility. 'Carnegie,' Johannson said, 'we've been right through the laboratory; dug up every piece of information we could find on Dance and Welles' tests –'

'And?'

'We've also analysed traces of the agent from the hypo they used on the suspect. I think we've found the *Boy*, Carnegie.'

'What boy?' Carnegie wanted to know; he found Johannson's obfuscation irritating.

'The *Blind Boy*, Carnegie.'

'And?'

For some inexplicable reason Carnegie was certain the man *smiled* down the phone before replying: 'I think perhaps you'd better come down and see for yourself. Sometime around noon suit you?'

Johannson could have been one of history's greatest poisoners: he had all the requisite qualifications. A tidy mind (poisoners were, in Carnegie's experience, domestic paragons), a patient nature (poison could take time), and, most importantly, an encyclopaedic knowledge of toxicology. Watching him at work, which Carnegie had done on two previous cases, was to see a subtle man at his subtle craft, and the spectacle made Carnegie's blood run cold.

Johannson had installed himself in the laboratory on the top floor, where Doctor Dance had been murdered, rather than use police facilities for the investigation, because, as he explained to Carnegie, much of the equipment the Hume organization boasted was simply not available elsewhere. His dominion over the place, accompanied by his two assistants had, however, transformed the laboratory from the clutter left by the experimenters, to a dream of order. Only the monkeys remained a constant. Try as he might Johannson could not control their behaviour.

'We didn't have much difficulty finding the drug used on your man,' Johannson said, 'we simply cross-checked traces remaining in the hypodermic with materials found in the room. In fact, they seem to have been manufacturing this stuff, or variations on the theme, for some time. The people here claim they know nothing about it, of course. I'm inclined to believe them. What the good doctors were doing here was, I'm sure, in the nature of a personal experiment.'

'What sort of experiment?'

Johannson took off his spectacles and set about cleaning them with the tongue of his red tie. 'At first, we thought they were developing some kind of hallucogen,' he said. 'In some regards the agent used on your man resembles a narcotic. In fact – methods apart – I think they made some very exciting discoveries. Developments which take us into entirely new territory.'

'It's not a drug then?'

'Oh, yes, of course it's a drug,' Johannson said, replacing the spectacles, 'but one created for a very specific purpose. See for yourself.'

Johannson led the way across the laboratory to the row of monkeys' cages. Instead of being confined separately, the toxicologist had seen fit to open the interconnecting doors between one cage and the next, allowing the animals free access to gather in groups. The consequence was absolutely plain: the animals were engaged in an elaborate series of sexual acts. Why, Carnegie wondered, did monkeys perpetually, perform obscenities? It was the same torrid display whenever he'd taken his offspring, as children, to Regent's Park Zoo; the Ape Enclosure elicited one embarrassing question upon another. He'd stopped taking the children after a while. He simply found it too mortifying.

'Haven't they got anything better to do?' he asked of Johannson, glancing away and then back at a menage à trois that was so intimate the eye could not ascribe member to monkey.

'Believe me,' Johannson smirked, 'this is mild by comparison with much of the behaviour we've seen from them since we gave them a shot of the agent. From that point on they neglected all normal behaviour patterns; they bypassed the arousal signals, the courtship rituals. They no longer show any interest in food. They don't sleep. They have become sexual obsessives. All other stimuli are forgotten. Unless the agent is naturally discharged, I suspect they are going to screw themselves to death.'

Carnegie looked along the rest of the cages: the same pornographic scenes were being played out in each one. Mass-rape, homosexual liaisons, fervent and ecstatic masturbation.

'It's no wonder the Doctors made a secret project of their discovery,' Johannson went on, 'they were on to something that could have made them a fortune. An aphrodisiac that actually works.'

'An aphrodisiac?'

'Most are useless, of course. Rhinoceros horn, live eels in cream sauce: symbolic stuff. They're designed to arouse by association.'

Carnegie remembered the hunger in Jerome's eyes. It was echoed here, in the monkeys'. Hunger, and the desperation that hunger brings.

'And the ointments too, all useless. *Cantharis vesticatora* –'

'What's that?'

'You know the stuff as Spanish Fly, perhaps? It's a paste made from a beetle. Again, useless. At best these things are inflammatants. But this . . . ' He picked up a phial of colourless fluid. '*This* is damn near genius.'

'They don't look too happy with it to me.'

'Oh, it's still crude,' Johannson said. 'I think the researchers were greedy, and moved into tests on living subjects a good two or three years before it was wise to do so. The stuff is almost lethal as it stands, no doubt of that. But it *could* be made to work, given time. You see, they've sidestepped the mechanical problems: this stuff operates directly on the sexual imagination, on the libido. If you arouse the *mind*, the body follows. That's the trick of it.'

A rattling of the wire-mesh close by drew Carnegie's attention from Johannson's pale features. One of the female monkeys, apparently not satisfied with the attentions of several males, was spreadeagled against her cage, her nimble fingers reaching for Carnegie; her spouses, not to be left loveless, had taken to sodomy. '*Blind Boy?*' said Carnegie. 'Is that Jerome?'

189

'It's Cupid, isn't it?' Johannson said: ' "*Love looks not with the eyes but with the mind,*

And therefore is winged Cupid painted blind".' It's *Midsummer Night's Dream*.'

'The Bard was never my strongest suit,' said Carnegie. He went back to staring at the female monkey. 'And Jerome?' he said.

'He has the agent in his system. A sizeable dose.'

'So he's like this lot!'

'I would presume – his intellectual capacities being greater – that the agent may not be able to work in quite such an *unfettered* fashion. But, having said that, sex can make monkeys out of the best of us, can't it?' Johannson allowed himself a half-smile at the notion. 'All our so-called higher concerns become secondary to the pursuit. For a short time sex makes us obsessive; we can perform, or at least *think* we can perform, what with hindsight may seem extraordinary feats.'

'I don't think there's anything so extraordinary about rape,' Carnegie commented, attempting to stem Johannson's rhapsody. But the other man would not be subdued.

'Sex without end, without compromise or apology,' he said. 'Imagine it. The dream of Casanova.'

The world had seen so many Ages. The Age of Enlightenment; of Reformation; of Reason. Now, at last, the Age of Desire. And after this, an end to Ages; an end, perhaps, to everything. For the fires that were being stoked now were fiercer than the innocent world suspected. They were terrible fires, fires without end, which would illuminate the world in one last, fierce light.

So Welles thought, as he lay in his bed. He had been conscious for several hours, but had chosen not to signify such. Whenever a nurse came to his room he would clamp his eyes closed and slow the rhythm of his breath. He knew he could not keep the illusion up for long, but the hours gave him a while to think through his itinerary from here. His first move had to be back to the Laboratories; there were papers there he had to shred; tapes to wipe clean. From now on he was determined that every scrap of information about *Project Blind Boy* exist solely in his head. That way he would have complete control over his masterwork, and nobody could claim it from him.

He had never had much interest in making money from the discovery, although he was well aware of how lucrative a workable aphrodisiac would be; he had never given a fig for material wealth. His initial motivation for the development of the drug – which they had chanced upon quite by accident while testing an agent to aid schizophrenics – had been investigative. But his motives had matured, through their months of secret work. He had come to think of himself as the bringer of the millenium. He would not have anyone attempt to snatch that sacred role from him.

So he thought, lying in his bed, waiting for a moment to slip away.

As he walked the streets Jerome would have happily yea-said Welles' vision. Perhaps he, of all men, was most eager to welcome the Age of Desire. He saw its portents everywhere. On advertising hoardings and cinema billboards, in shop-windows, on television screens: everywhere, the body as merchandise. Where flesh was not being used to market artifacts of steel and stone, those artifacts were taking on its properties. Automobiles passed him by with every voluptuous attribute but breath: their sinuous body-work gleamed, their interiors invited, plushly; the buildings beleaguered him with sexual puns. Spires; passageways; shadowed plazas with white-water fountains. Beneath the raptures of the shallow – the thousand trivial distractions he encountered in street and square – he sensed the ripe life of the body informing every particular.

The spectacle kept the fire in him well-stoked; it was all that will power could do to keep him from pressing his attentions on every creature that he met eyes with. A few seemed to sense the heat in him, and gave him wide berth. Dogs sensed it too. Several followed him, aroused by *his* arousal. Flies orbited his head in squadrons. But his growing ease with his condition gave him some rudimentary control over it. He knew that to make a public display of his ardour would bring the law down upon him, and that in turn would hinder his adventures. Soon enough, the fire that he had begun would spread: *then* he would emerge from hiding and bathe in it freely. Until then, discretion was best.

He had on occasion bought the company of a young woman in Soho; he went to find her now. The afternoon was stiflingly hot, but he felt no weariness. He had not eaten since the previous evening, but he felt no hunger. Indeed, as he climbed the narrow stairway up to the room on the first floor which Angela had once occupied, he felt as primed as an athlete, glowing with health. The immaculately dressed and wall-eyed pimp who usually occupied a place at the top of the stairs was absent. Jerome simply went to the girl's room and knocked. There was no reply. He rapped again, more urgently. The noise brought an early middle-aged woman to the door at the end of the landing.

'What do you want?'

'The woman,' he replied simply.

'Angela's gone. And you'd better get out of here too, in that state. This isn't a doss-house.'

'When will she be back?' he asked, keeping as tight a leash as he could on his appetite.

The woman, who was as tall as Jerome and half as heavy again as his wasted frame, advanced towards him. 'The girl won't *be* back,' she said, 'so you get the hell out of here, before I call Isaiah.'

Jerome looked at the woman; she shared Angela's profession, no doubt, if not her youth or prettiness. He smiled at her. 'I can hear your heart,' he said.

'I told you –'

Before she could finish the words Jerome moved down the landing towards her. She wasn't intimidated by his approach, merely repulsed.

'If I call Isaiah, you'll be sorry,' she informed him. The pace of her heartbeat had risen, he could hear it.

'I'm burning,' he said.

She frowned; she was clearly losing this battle of wits. 'Stay away from me,' she told. 'I'm warning you.'

The heartbeat was getting more rapid still. The rhythm, buried in her substance, drew him on. From that source: all life, all heat.

'Give me your heart,' he said.

'Isaiah!'

Nobody came running at her shout, however. Jerome gave her no opportunity to cry out a second time. He reached to embrace her, clamping a hand over her mouth. She let fly a volley of blows against him, but the pain only fanned the flames. He was brighter by the moment: his every orifice let on to the furnace in belly and loins and head. Her superior bulk was of no advantage against such fervour. He pushed her against the wall – the beat of her heart loud in his ears – and began to apply kisses to her neck, tearing her dress open to free her breasts.

'Don't shout,' he said, trying to sound persuasive. 'There's no harm meant.'

She shook her head, and said, 'I won't,' against his palm. He took his hand from her mouth, and she dragged in several desperate breaths. Where was Isaiah? she thought. Not far, surely. Fearing for her life if she tried to resist this interloper – how his eyes shone! – she gave up any pretence to resistance and let him have his way. Men's supply of passion, she knew of long experience, was easily depleted. Though they might threaten to move earth and heaven too, half an hour later their boasts would be damp sheets and resentment. If the worst came to the worst, she could tolerate his inane talk of burning; she'd heard far obscener bedroom chat. As to the prong he was even now attempting to press into her, it and its comical like held no surprises for her.

Jerome wanted to touch the heart in her; wanted to see it splash up into his face, to bathe in it. He put his hand to her breast, and felt the beat of her under his palm.

'You like that, do you?' she said as he pressed against her bosom. 'You're not the first.'

He clawed her skin.

'Gently, sweetheart,' she chided him, looking over his shoulder to see if there was any sign of Isaiah. 'Be gentle. This is the only body I've got.'

He ignored her. His nails drew blood.

'Don't do that,' she said.

'Wants to be out,' he replied digging deeply, and it suddenly dawned on her that this was no love-game he was playing.

'*Stop it*,' she said, as he began to tear at her. This time, she screamed.

Downstairs, and a short way along the street, Isaiah dropped the slice of *tarte française* he'd just bought and ran to the door. It wasn't the first time his sweet tooth had tempted him from his post, but – unless he was quick to undo the damage – it might very well be his last. There were terrible noises from the landing. He raced up the stairs. The scene that met his eyes was in every way

194

worse than that his imagination had conjured. Simone was trapped against the wall beside her door, with a man battened upon her. Blood was coming from somewhere between them, he couldn't see where.

Isaiah yelled. Jerome, hands bloody, looked round from his labours as a giant in a Savile Row suit reached for him. It took Jerome vital seconds to uproot himself from the furrow, by which time the man was upon him. Isaiah took hold of him, and dragged him off the woman. She took shelter, sobbing, in her room.

'Sick bastard,' Isaiah said, launching a fusillade of punches. Jerome reeled. But he was on fire, and unafraid. In a moment's respite he leapt at his man like an angered baboon. Isaiah, taken unawares, lost balance, and fell back against one of the doors, which opened inwards against his weight. He collapsed into a squalid lavatory, his head striking the lip of the toilet bowl as he went down. The impact disoriented him, and he lay on the stained linoleum groaning, legs akimbo. Jerome could hear his blood, eager in his veins; could smell sugar on his breath. It tempted him to stay. But his instinct for self-preservation counselled otherwise; Isaiah was already making an attempt to stand up again. Before he could get to his feet Jerome about turned, and made a getaway down the stairs.

The dog-day met him at the doorstep, and he smiled. The street wanted him more than the woman on the landing, and he was eager to oblige. He started out on to the pavement, his erection still pressing from his trousers. Behind him, he heard the giant pounding down the stairs. He took to his heels, laughing. The fire was still uncurbed in him, and it lent speed to his feet; he ran down the street not caring if Sugar Breath was following or not. Pedestrians, unwilling, in this dispassionate age, to register more than casual interest in the blood-spattered satyr, parted to let him pass. A few pointed, assuming him an actor perhaps. Most took no notice at all. He made his way through a maze of back streets, aware without needing to look that Isaiah was still on his heels.

Perhaps it was accident that brought him to the street market; perhaps, and more probably, it was that the swelter carried the mingled scent of meat and fruit to his nostrils, and he wanted to bathe in it. The narrow thoroughfare was thronged with purchasers, sightseers, and stalls heaped with merchandise. He dove into the crowd happily, brushing against buttock and thigh, meeting the plaguing gaze of fellow flesh on every side. Such a day! He and his prick could scarcely believe their luck.

Behind him, he heard Isaiah shout. He picked up his pace, heading for the most densely populated areas of the market, where he could lose himself in the hot press of people. Each contact was a painful ecstasy. Each climax – and they came one upon the other as he pressed through the crowd – was a dry spasm in his system. His back ached, his balls ached: but what his body now? Just a plinth for that singular monument, his prick. Head was *nothing*; mind was *nothing*. His arms were simply made to bring love close, his legs to carry the demanding rod any place where it might find satisfaction. He pictured himself as a walking erection, the world gaping on every side: flesh, brick, steel, he didn't care: he would ravish it all.

Suddenly, without his seeking it, the crowd parted, and he found himself off the main thoroughfare and in a narrow street. Sunlight poured between the buildings, its zeal magnified. He was about to turn back to join the crowd again when he caught a scent and sight that drew him on. A short way down the heat-drenched street three shirtless young men were standing amid piles of fruit crates, each containing dozens of punnets

196

of strawberries. There had been a glut of the fruit that year, and in the relentless heat much of it had begun to soften and rot. The trio of workers was going through the punnets, sorting bad fruit from good, and throwing the spoiled strawberries into the gutter. The smell in the narrow space was overpowering: a sweetness of such strength it would have sickened any interloper other than Jerome, whose senses had lost all capacity for revulsion or rejection. The world was the world was the world; he would take it, as in marriage, for better or worse. He stood watching the spectacle entranced; the sweating fruit-sorters bright in the fall of sun, hands, arms and torsoes spattered with scarlet juice; the air mazed with every nectar-seeking insect; the discarded fruit heaped in the gutter in seeping mounds. Engaged in their sticky labours the sorters didn't even see him at first. Then one of the three looked up, and took in the extraordinary creature watching them. The grin on his face died as he met Jerome's eyes.

'What the hell?'

Now the other two looked up from their work.

'Sweet,' said Jerome; he could hear their hearts tremble.

'Look at him,' said the youngest of the three, pointing at Jerome's groin. 'Fucking exposing himself.'

They stood still in the sunlight, he and they, while the wasps whirled around the fruit, and, in the narrow slice of blue summer sky between the roofs, birds passed over. Jerome wanted the moment to go on forever: his too-naked head tasted Eden here.

And then, the dream broke. He felt a shadow on his back. One of the sorters dropped the punnet he was sorting through; the decayed fruit broke open on the gravel. Jerome frowned, and half-turned. Isaiah had found the street; his weapon was steel and shone. It crossed the space between he and Jerome in one short

197

second. Jerome felt an ache in his side as the knife slid into him.

'*Christ*,' the young man said, and began to run; his two brothers, unwilling to be witnesses at the scene of a wounding, hesitated only moments longer before following.

The pain made Jerome cry out, but nobody in the noisy market heard him. Isaiah withdrew the blade; heat came with it. He made to stab again, but Jerome was too fast for the spoiler; he moved out of range and staggered across the street. The would-be assassin, fearful that Jerome's cries would draw too much attention, moved quickly in pursuit to finish the job. But the tarmac was slick with rotted fruit, and his fine suede shoes had less grip than Jerome's bare feet. The gap between them widened by a pace.

'No you don't,' Isaiah said, determined not to let his humiliator escape. He pushed over a tower of fruit crates – punnets toppled and strewed their contents across Jerome's path. Jerome hesitated, to take in the bouquet of bruised fruit. The indulgence almost killed him. Isaiah closed in, ready to take the man. Jerome, his system taxed to near eruption by the stimulus of pain, watched the blade come close to opening up his belly. His mind conjured the wound: the abdomen slit – the heat spilling out to join the blood of the strawberries in the gutter. The thought was so tempting. He almost wanted it.

Isaiah had killed before, twice. He knew the wordless vocabulary of the act, and he could see the invitation in his victim's eyes. Happy to oblige, he came to meet it, knife at the ready. At the last possible moment Jerome recanted, and instead of presenting himself for slitting, threw a blow at the giant. Isaiah ducked to avoid it and his feet slid in the mush. The knife fled from his hand and fell amongst the debris of punnets and fruit.

198

Jerome turned away as the hunter – the advantage lost – stooped to locate the knife. But his prey was gone before his ham-fisted grip had found it: lost again in the crowd-filled streets. He had no opportunity to pocket the knife before the uniform stepped out of the crowd and joined him in the hot passageway.

'What's the story?' the policeman demanded, looking down at the knife. Isaiah followed his gaze. The bloodied blade was black with flies.

In his office Inspector Carnegie sipped at his hot chocolate, his third in the past hour, and watched the processes of dusk. He had always wanted to be a detective, right from his earliest rememberings; and, in those rememberings, this had always been a charged and magical hour. Night descending on the city; myriad evils putting on their glad rags and coming out to play. A time for vigilance, for a new moral stringency.

But as a child he had failed to imagine the fatigue that twilight invariably brought. He was tired to his bones, and if he snatched any sleep in the next few hours he knew it would be here, in his chair, with his feet up on the desk amid a clutter of plastic cups.

The phone rang. It was Johannson.

'Still at work?' he said, impressed by Johannson's dedication to the job. It was well after nine. Perhaps Johannson didn't have a home worth calling such to go back to either.

'I heard our man had a busy day,' Johannson said.

'That's right. A prostitute in Soho; then got himself stabbed.'

'He got through the cordon, I gather?'

'These things happen,' Carnegie replied, too tired to be testy. 'What can I do for you?'

'I just thought you'd want to know: the monkeys have started to die.'

The words stirred Carnegie from his fatigue-stupor. 'How many?' he asked.

'Three from fourteen so far. But the rest will be dead by dawn, I'd guess.'

'What's killing them? Exhaustion?' Carnegie recalled the desperate saturnalia he'd seen in the cages. What animal – human or otherwise – could keep up such revelry without cracking up?

'It's not physical,' Johannson said. 'Or at least not in the way you're implying. We'll have to wait for the dissection results before we get any detailed explanations –'

'Your best guess?'

'For what it's worth . . .' Johannson said, '. . . which is quite a lot: I think they're going *bang*.'

'What?'

'Cerebral over-load of some kind. Their brains are simply giving out. The agent doesn't disperse you see; *it feeds on itself*. The more fevered they get, the more of the drug is produced; the more of the drug there is, the more fevered they get. It's a vicious circle. Hotter and hotter, wilder and wilder. Eventually the system can't take it, and suddenly I'm up to my armpits in dead monkeys.' The smile came back into the voice again, cold and wry. 'Not that the others let that spoil their fun. Necrophilia's quite the fashion down here.'

Carnegie peered at his cooling hot chocolate; it had acquired a thin skin, which puckered as he touched the cup. 'So it's just a matter of time?' he said.

'Before our man goes for bust? Yes, I'd think so.'

'All right. Thank you for the up-date. Keep me posted.'

'You want to come down here and view the remains?'

'Monkey corpses I can do without, thank you.'

Johannson laughed. Carnegie put down the receiver. When he turned back to the window, night had well and truly fallen.

In the laboratory Johannson crossed to the light switch by the door; in the time he'd been calling Carnegie the last of the daylight had fled. He saw the blow that felled him coming a mere heartbeat before it landed; it caught him across the side of his neck. One of his vertebrae snapped, and his legs buckled. He collapsed without reaching the lightswitch. But by the time he hit the ground the distinction between day and night was academic.

Welles didn't bother to check whether his blow had been lethal or not; time was at a premium. He stepped over the body and headed across to the bench where Johannson had been working. There, lying in a circle of lamplight as if for the final act of a simian tragedy, lay a dead monkey. It had clearly perished in a frenzy; its face was knitted up: mouth wide and spittle-stained, eyes fixed in a final look of alarm. Its fur had been pulled out in tufts in the throes of its copulations; its body, wasted with exertion, was a mass of contusions. It took Welles half a minute of study to recognize the implications of the corpse, and of the other two he now saw lying on a nearby bench.

'Love kills,' he murmured to himself philosophically, and began his systematic destruction of *Blind Boy*.

I'm dying, Jerome thought, I'm dying of *terminal joy*. The thought amused him. It was the only thought in his head which made much sense. Since his encounter with Isaiah, and the escape from the police that had followed, he could remember little with any coherence. The hours of hiding and nursing his wounds – of feeling the heat grow again, and of discharging it – had long

201

since merged into one midsummer dream, from which, he knew with pleasurable certainty, only death would wake him. The blaze was devouring him utterly, from the entrails out. If he were to be eviscerated now, what would the witnesses find? Only embers and ashes.

Yet still his one-eyed friend demanded *more*; still, as he wove his way back to the Laboratories – where else for a made man to go when the stitches slipped, but back to the first heat? – still the grids gaped at him seductively, and every brick wall offered up a hundred gritty invitations.

The night was balmy: a night for love-songs and romance. In the questionable privacy of a parking lot a few blocks from his destination he saw two people making sex in the back of a car, the doors open to accommodate limbs and draught. Jerome paused to watch the ritual, enthralled as ever by the tangle of bodies, and the sound – so loud it was like thunder – of twin hearts beating to one escalating rhythm. Watching, his rod grew eager.

The female saw him first, and alerted her partner to the wreck of a human being who was watching them with such childish delight. The male looked around from his gropings to stare. Do I burn, Jerome wondered? Does my hair flame? At the last, does the illusion gain substance? To judge by the look on their faces, the answer was surely no. They were not in awe of him, merely angered and revolted.

'I'm on fire,' he told them.

The male got to his feet and spat at Jerome. He almost expected the spittle to turn to steam as it approached him but instead it landed on his face and upper chest as a cooling shower.

'Go to hell,' the woman said. 'Leave us alone.'

Jerome shook his head. The male warned him that another step would oblige him to break Jerome's head.

It disturbed our man not a jot; no words, no blows, could silence the imperative of the rod.

Their hearts, he realized, as he moved towards them, no longer beat in tandem.

Carnegie consulted the map, five years out of date now, on his office wall, to pinpoint the location of the attack that had just been reported. Neither of the victims had come to serious harm, apparently; the arrival of a car-load of revellers had dissuaded Jerome (it was unquestionably Jerome) from lingering. Now the area was being flooded with officers, half a dozen of them armed; in a matter of minutes every street in the vicinity of the attack would be cordoned off. Unlike Soho, which had been crowded, the area would furnish the fugitive with few hiding places.

Carnegie pin-pointed the location of the attack, and realised that it was within a few blocks of the Laboratories. No accident, surely. The man was heading back to the scene of his crime. Wounded, and undoubtedly on the verge of collapse – the lovers had described a man who looked more dead than alive – Jerome would probably be picked up before he reached home. But there was always the risk of his slipping through the net, and getting to the Laboratories. Johannson was working there, alone; the guard on the building was, in these straitened times, necessarily small.

Carnegie picked up the phone and dialled through to Johannson. The phone rang at the other end, but nobody picked it up. The man's gone home, Carnegie thought, happy to be relieved of his concern, it's ten-fifty at night and he's earned his rest. Just as he was about to put the receiver down, however, it was picked up at the other end.

'Johannson?'

Nobody replied.

'Johannson? This is Carnegie.' And still, no reply. 'Answer me, damn it. Who is this?'

In the Laboratories the receiver was forsaken. It was not replaced on the cradle but left to lie on the bench. Down the buzzing line, Carnegie could clearly hear the monkeys, their voices shrill.

'Johannson?' Carnegie demanded. 'Are you there? Johannson?'

But the apes screamed on.

Welles had built two bonfires of the *Blind Boy* material in the sinks, and then set them alight. They flared up enthusiastically. Smoke, heat and smuts filled the large room, thickening the air. When the fires were fairly raging he threw all the tapes he could lay hands upon into the conflagration, and added all of Johannson's notes for good measure. Several of the tapes had already gone from the files, he noted. But all they could show any thief was some teasing scenes of transformation: the heart of the secret remained his. With the procedures and formulae now destroyed, it only remained to wash the small amounts of remaining agent down the drain, and kill and incinerate the animals.

He prepared a series of lethal hypodermics, going about the business with uncharacteristic orderliness. This systematic destruction gratified him. He felt no regret at the way things had turned out. From that first moment of panic, when he'd helplessly watched the *Blind Boy* serum work its awesome effects upon Jerome – to this final elimination of all that had gone before – had been, he now saw, one steady process of wiping clean. With these fires he brought an end to the pretence of scientific enquiry; after this he was indisputably the Apostle of Desire, its John in the wilderness. The thought blinded him to any other.

Careless of the monkeys' scratchings he hauled them one by one, from their cages to deliver the killing dose. He had dispatched three, and was opening the cage of the fourth, when a figure appeared in the doorway of the laboratory. Through the smoky air it was impossible to see who. The surviving monkeys seemed to recognize him, however: they left off their couplings and set up a din of welcome.

Welles stood still, and waited for the newcomer to make his move.

'I'm dying,' said Jerome.

Welles had not expected this. Of all the people he had anticipated here, Jerome was the last.

'Did you hear me?' the man wanted to know.

Welles nodded. 'We're *all* dying, Jerome. Life is a slow disease, no more nor less. But such a *light*, eh? in the going.'

'You *knew* this would happen,' Jerome said. 'You knew the fire would eat me away.'

'No,' came the sober reply. 'No, I didn't. Really.'

Jerome walked out of the door frame and into the murky light. He was a wasted shambles: a patchwork man, blood on his body, fire in his eyes. But Welles knew better than to trust the apparent vulnerability of this scarecrow. The agent in his system had made him capable of superhuman acts: he had seen Dance torn open with a few nonchalant strokes. Tact was required. Though clearly close to death, Jerome was still formidable.

'I didn't intend this, Jerome,' Welles said, attempting to tame the tremor in his voice. 'I wish, in a way, I could claim that I had. But I wasn't that far-sighted. It's taken me time and pain to see the future plainly.'

The burning man watched him, gaze intent.

'Such fires, Jerome, waiting to be lit.'

'I know . . .' Jerome replied. 'Believe me . . . I know.'

'You and I; we are the end of the world.'

The wretched monster pondered this for a while, and then nodded slowly. Welles softly exhaled a sigh of relief; the death-bed diplomacy was working. But he had little time to waste with talk. If Jerome was here, could the authorities be far behind?

'I have urgent work to do, my friend,' he said calmly. 'Would you think me uncivil if I continued with it?'

Without waiting for a reply he unlatched another cage and hauled the condemned monkey out, expertly turning its body round to facilitate the injection. The animal convulsed in his arms for a few moments, then died. Welles disengaged its wizened fingers from his shirt, and tossed the corpse and the discharged hypodermic on to the bench, turning with an executioner's economy to claim his next victim.

'Why?' Jerome asked, staring at the animal's open eyes.

'Act of mercy,' Welles replied, picking up another primed hypodermic. 'You can see how they're suffering.' He reached to unlatch the next cage.

'Don't,' Jerome said.

'No time for sentiment,' Welles replied. 'I beg you: an end to that.'

Sentiment, Jerome thought, muddily remembering the songs on the radio that had first rewoken the fire in him. Didn't Welles understand that the processes of heart and head and groin were indivisible? That sentiment, however trite, might lead to undiscovered regions? He wanted to tell the Doctor that, to explain all that he had seen and all that he had loved in these desperate hours. But somewhere between mind and tongue the explanations absconded. All he could say, to state the empathy he felt for all the suffering world, was:

'*Don't*,' as Welles unlocked the next cage. The Doctor ignored him, and reached into the wire-mesh cell. It contained three animals. He took hold of the nearest and drew it, protesting, from its companions' embraces. Without doubt it knew what fate awaited it; a flurry of screeches signalled its terror.

Jerome couldn't stomach this casual disposal. He moved, the wound in his side a torment, to prevent the killing. Welles, distracted by Jerome's advance, lost hold of his wriggling charge: the monkey scampered away across the bench-tops. As he went to re-capture it the prisoners in the cage behind him took their chance, and slipped out.

'Damn you,' Welles yelled at Jerome, 'don't you see we've no *time*? Don't you understand?'

Jerome understood everything, and yet nothing. The fever he and the animals shared, he understood; its purpose, to transform the world, he understood too. But why it should end like this – that joy, that vision – why it should all come down to a sordid room filled with smoke and pain, to frailty, to despair – *that* he did not comprehend. Nor, he now realized, did Welles, who had been the architect of these contradictions.

As the Doctor made a snatch for one of the escaping monkeys, Jerome crossed swiftly to the remaining cages and unlatched them all: the animals leapt to their freedom. Welles had succeeded with his recapture however, and had the protesting monkeys in his grip, about to deliver the panacea. Jerome made towards him.

'Let it be,' he yelled.

Welles pressed the hypodermic into the monkey's body, but before he could depress the plunger Jerome had pulled at his wrist. The hypodermic spat its poison into the air, and then fell to the ground: the monkey, wresting itself free, followed.

207

Jerome pulled Welles close. 'I told you to *let it be*,' he said.

Welles' response was to drive his fist into Jerome's wounded flank. Tears of pain spurted from his eyes, but he didn't release the Doctor. The stimulus, unpleasant as it was, could not dissuade him from holding that beating heart close. He wished, embracing Welles like a prodigal, that he could ignite himself: that the dream of burning flesh he had endured would now become a reality, consuming maker and made in one cleansing flame. But his flesh was only flesh; his bone, bone. What miracles he had seen had been a private revelation, and now there was no time to communicate their glories or their horrors. What he had seen would die with him, to be rediscovered (perhaps) by some future self, only to be forgotten and discovered again. Like the story of love the radio had told; the same joy lost and found, found and lost. He stared at Welles with new comprehension dawning, hearing still the terrified beat of the man's heart. The Doctor was *wrong*. If he left the man to live, he would come to know his error. They were not presagers of the millenium. They had both been dreaming.

'Don't kill me,' Welles pleaded. 'I don't want to die.'

More fool you, Jerome thought, and let the man go.

Welles' bafflement was plain: he couldn't believe that his appeal for life had been answered. Anticipating a blow with every step he took, he backed away from Jerome, who simply turned his back on the Doctor and walked away.

From downstairs there came a shout, and then many shouts. Police, Welles guessed. They had presumably found the body of the officer who'd been on guard at the door. In moments only they would be coming up the stairs. There was no time now for finishing the

208

tasks he'd come here to perform. He had to be away before they arrived.

On the floor below, Carnegie watched the armed officers disappear up the stairs. There was a faint smell of burning in the air; he feared the worst.

I am the man who comes after the act, he thought to himself; I am perpetually upon the scene when the best of the action is over. Used as he was to waiting, patient as a loyal dog, this time he could not hold his anxieties in check while the others went ahead. Disregarding the voices advising him to wait, he began up the stairs.

The laboratory on the top floor was empty, but for the monkeys and Johannson's corpse. The toxicologist lay on his face where he had fallen, neck broken. The emergency exit, which let on to the fire-escape, was open; smoky air was being sucked out through it. As Carnegie stepped away from Johannson's body officers were already on the fire-escape, calling to their colleagues below to seek out the fugitive.

'Sir?'

Carnegie looked across at the moustachioed individual who had approached him.

'What is it?'

The officer pointed to the other end of the laboratory: to the test-chamber. There was somebody at the window. Carnegie recognized the features, even though they were much changed. It was Jerome. At first he thought the man was watching him, but a short perusal scotched that idea. Jerome was staring, tears on his face, at his own reflection in the smeared glass. Even as Carnegie watched, the face retreated with the gloom of the chamber.

Other officers had noticed the man too. They were moving down the length of the laboratory, taking up positions behind the benches where they had a good line on the door, weapons at the ready. Carnegie had been present in such situations before; they had their own, terrible momentum. Unless he intervened, there would be blood.

'No,' he said, 'hold your fire.'

He pressed the protesting officer aside and began to walk down the laboratory, making no attempt to conceal his advance. He walked past sinks in which the remains of *Blind Boy* guttered, past the bench under which, a short age ago, they'd found the dead Dance. A monkey, its head bowed, dragged itself across his path, apparently deaf to his proximity. He let it find a hole to die in, then moved on to the chamber door. It was ajar. He reached for the handle. Behind him the laboratory had fallen completely silent; all eyes were on him. He pulled the door open. Fingers tightened on triggers. There was no attack however. Carnegie stepped inside.

Jerome was standing against the opposite wall. If he saw Carnegie enter, or heard him, he made no sign of it. A dead monkey lay at his feet, one hand still grasping the hem of his trousers. Another whimpered in the corner, holding its head in its hands.

'Jerome?'

Was it Carnegie's imagination, or could he smell strawberries?

Jerome blinked.

'You're under arrest,' Carnegie said. Hendrix would appreciate the irony of that, he thought. The man moved his bloody hand from the stabwound in his side to the front of his trousers, and began to stroke himself.

'Too late,' Jerome said. He could feel the last fire rising in him. Even if this intruder chose to cross the chamber and arrest him now, the intervening seconds would deny him his capture. *Death was here*. And what was it, now he saw it clearly? Just another seduction, another sweet darkness to be filled up, and pleasured and made fertile.

210

A spasm began in his perineum, and lightning travelled in two directions from the spot, up his rod and up his spine. A laugh began in his throat.

In the corner of the chamber the monkey, hearing Jerome's humour, began to whimper again. The sound momentarily claimed Carnegie's attention, and when his gaze flitted back to Jerome the short-sighted eyes had closed, the hand had dropped, and he was dead, standing against the wall. For a short time the body defied gravity. Then, gracefully the legs buckled and Jerome fell forward. He was, Carnegie saw, a sack of bones, no more. It was a wonder the man had lived so long.

Cautiously, he crossed to the body and put his finger to the man's neck. There was no pulse. The remnants of Jerome's last laugh remained on his face, however, refusing to decay.

'Tell me . . .' Carnegie whispered to the man, sensing that despite his pre-emption he had missed the moment; that once again he was, and perhaps would always be, merely a witness of consequences. 'Tell me. *What was the joke?*'

But the blind boy, as is the wont of his clan, wasn't telling.

THE DAMNATION GAME

Clive Barker

'It was an odd disease. Its symptoms were like infatuation
– palpitations, sleeplessness. Its only certain cure,
Death . . .'

Chance had ruled Marty Strauss' life for as long as he
could remember. Now at last luck was turning his way.

Parolled from prison, he becomes bodyguard to Joseph
Whitehead, one of the richest men in Europe.

But Whitehead has also played with chance – an ancient
game which gave him vast power and wealth, in exchange
for his immortal soul.

Now the forces he played against are back to claim what's
theirs. Terrifying forces, with the power to raise the dead;
and Marty is trapped between his human masters and
Hell itself, with just one last, desperate game left to
play . . .

'I think Clive Barker is so good that I am almost literally
tongue-tied'
Stephen King

'Clive Barker writes about horrors most of us would
scarcely dare imagine'
Ramsey Campbell

'The most impressive first novel I've read for a long, long
time. Touches of sheer brilliance throughout'
James Herbert

Also by Clive Barker in Sphere Books:
BOOKS OF BLOOD volumes 1–6